Elvis, Me, and the Lemonade Stand Summer

Leslie Gentile

DCB

Canada Council for the Arts   Conseil des Arts du Canada

ONTARIO ARTS COUNCIL
CONSEIL DES ARTS DE L'ONTARIO
an Ontario government agency
un organisme du gouvernement de l'Ontario

Canadian Heritage   Patrimoine canadien

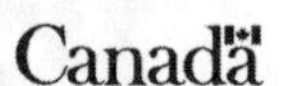

The publisher gratefully acknowledges the support of the Canada Council for the Arts and the Ontario Arts Council for its publishing program. We acknowledge the financial support of the Government of Canada through the Canada Book Fund (CBF) for our publishing activities, and the Government of Ontario through Ontario Creates, an agency of the Ontario Ministry of Culture, and the Ontario Book Publishing Tax Credit Program.

LIBRARY AND ARCHIVES CANADA CATALOGUING IN PUBLICATION

Title: Elvis, me, and the lemonade stand summer / Leslie Gentile.
Names: Gentile, Leslie, 1959– author.
Identifiers: Canadiana (print) 20200342657 | Canadiana (ebook) 2020034269X | ISBN 9781770866157 (softcover) | ISBN 9781770866164 (HTML)
Classification: LCC PS8613.E5555 E48 2021 | DDC JC813/.6—dc23

United States Library of Congress Control Number: 2020950455

Cover art: Julie McLaughlin
Interior text design: Tannice Goddard, tannicegdesigns.ca

Printed and bound in Canada.
Manufactured by Friesens in Altona, Manitoba in February 2021.

DCB Young Readers
AN IMPRINT OF CORMORANT BOOKS INC.
260 SPADINA AVENUE, SUITE 502, TORONTO, ONTARIO, M5T 2E4
www.dcbyoungreaders.com
www.cormorantbooks.com

This book is dedicated to:

My mother, who taught me to dream.
Dan, who always champions my writing.
Aimes, Lyse & Tristan,
who always believed I could do it.
My grandchildren Sadie, Charlotte & Declan,
the next generation of dreamers.

CHAPTER 1

The summer Elvis came into my life he drove right up to my lemonade stand in a Volkswagen — a gold-colored Sun Bug Super Beetle. And nothing was ever the same after that.

Okay, so it might not have been the real Elvis. After all, it had been widely reported that he had been dead for almost a year. But then, you never really know for sure, right? A lot of magazines and newspapers at the Food Mart checkout claimed that he was still alive, and every once in a while, he was photographed hanging out in places like laundromats. So it was entirely possible that he had pulled up to my lemonade stand in a gold Sun Bug.

And this guy sure looked like Elvis. Sounded like him. And acted like him. Or how I imagined Elvis would act, if he got to live like a normal person and showed up for a glass of lemonade at a stand in front of a run-down trailer park on an Indian reserve.

So here's how the summer started. Andy El insisted that

I set up a lemonade stand on the side of the road in front of our trailer park. She hauled out an old piece of plywood and set it up on some rickety old sawhorses that she'd found lying out in the junk pile behind the shed beside her trailer. It looked pretty bad, even to Andy El, who is always so darned positive about everything, so she covered it with an old tablecloth she didn't mind me using outdoors.

Which is how I ended up with a Christmas tablecloth with dancing snowmen on it to cover my lemonade stand. Years before, someone had embroidered "Have a Cool Yule Y'all!" in green thread along the frayed edges. And while it was festive, it did not exactly scream "lemonade stand."

Andy El had even invested in six cans of lemonade to get me started, let me borrow her blue plastic juice jug and some mismatched plastic glasses, and provided ice cubes from the metal tray in the old fridge she kept out on her back porch. So I really didn't have much choice in the end. I tried to tell her that at eleven years old I was way too old for running a lemonade stand, but she just smiled, ignored my complaints, and kept setting it up.

Her name is really Ella Charlie, and she owns the trailer park. When I was little, just learning to walk around on the uneven ground in the trailer park, I heard all her relatives calling her Auntie Ella. I thought they were saying "Andy El." Somehow the name caught on, and now everyone, even her family, calls her that. Even her grown nephew Raymond and her daughter Esther, although sometimes they call her Mama.

Andy El is Coast Salish. Clarice — my mom — is white, but I know that my dad is an Indian. Clarice has never bothered to tell me anything about him, so this is just guesswork on my part. As a natural blonde, Clarice sunburns easily and has "fine,delicate features," as she likes to say. I have darker skin and hair, am short and a bit stocky. So I figure I must take after my dad, and the only thing I know about him is that he must be Native.

Anyways. Andy El is the nicest, kindest person I've ever met, and is always cheerful. She sees the best in people. She also keeps an eye out for me, and she's always been someone I could count on ever since my mom and I moved in to the trailer park. Which is a good thing, because one thing Clarice cannot be called is maternal.

So, Day One of the lemonade stand, and there I was, miserable, bored, sitting in the hot sun at my stand, watching the ice melt in the jug of lemonade on the rickety, makeshift table in front of me.

No one will stop. No one ever drives down this road, I told myself.

Just then, to prove me wrong, that Volkswagen Sun Bug turned at the four-way stop and headed toward me. That stretch of road ran flat and straight, so I sat and watched the Sun Bug's progress as it made its way down toward Eagle Shores. I held my breath and watched as the gold car approached, slowed, and stopped in front of my table.

Now I'll never hear the end of it from Andy El, I thought. I had tried to tell her that it wouldn't work out, because one thing I knew about life for sure — nothing ever worked out for me. But she'd cheerfully insisted and had finally worn me down.

"You need something to do this summer. It'll be fun, you'll see," she'd said as she kept setting things up. "You can earn some money for yourself. Save up for something special, maybe."

And here I was, with my first customer driving up in a Volkswagen Beetle.

The car stopped, the driver's door opened, and out he stepped. It was the King. Elvis Presley. With aviator sunglasses, black hair, big sideburns, and all.

He stretched as though he'd been stuck behind the wheel of that Bug for hours, then looked down at me and smiled.

"How much?" he asked in a quiet drawl.

I just sat there and stared stupidly at him. He took off his sunglasses and smiled at me with the bluest eyes I have ever seen.

"How much? For a glass of lemonade?" he asked again. Polite, like all the magazines said he was.

I just pointed to the sign, which read: *Lemonaid 10 cents.* I had half-heartedly made the sign that morning. It was only after I'd opened the can of lemonade and read the label that I discovered that I'd spelled it wrong. Up until now I hadn't cared. I didn't think that anyone would stop at my stand, much less notice my misspelled sign. Not this far off the beaten track, down an unpaved road that led past a couple of ramshackle fruit farms and ended at the Eagle Shores Trailer Park. On the edge of the Eagle Shores Indian Reserve.

I was pretty sure I knew why Andy El had insisted I set up the stand. It was to give me something to do through this whole long, hot, boring summer, since she knew I had nothing to look forward to at the trailer park.

My family was just me and my mom. Clarice and I rented a trailer from Andy El, and had done ever since I could remember. Andy El has a small patch of ground that was part of the Eagle Shores Indian Reserve on southern Vancouver Island, and years ago she and her husband had set up a small trailer park of fifteen trailers. After her husband died, Andy El just kept it going. Some of the trailers were owned outright by people who paid her a monthly fee to keep their trailer there, and a few were owned by Andy El. Those ones she rents out.

Anyways, Andy El knew that I wouldn't have a summer like the other kids at my school, who all had plans to go to summer camp, swimming and sailing lessons, sleepovers, and all sorts of fun-filled days and nights.

All the great-sounding stuff the other kids chattered excitedly about on the last day of school and on the long bus ride home. I just sat, staring out the window, glumly listening as they all made plans with their friends to meet at the local lake to go swimming, or share a cabin at summer camp, or some other great time. I'm not going to lie: I felt sorry for myself, and maybe even a little bit jealous.

And I knew that Andy El wanted me to have something to do, since she knew that Clarice had a new boyfriend, and that meant that I was even less important than before to my mom. They were in what Clarice called the "honeymoon stage of a relationship," which meant that I would have to "keep a low profile" till she broke it to the new guy that she had a kid. A kid my age, eleven. Turning twelve in August.

"It's nothin' personal, kiddo, but it cramps my style, ya know? It can turn a guy off to know that there's a kid in the picture," she'd explained. "I just need to work my charms for a while, till I hook him in, and then ..." She laughed and pretended to cast an imaginary fishing rod in the air, and mimed reeling in the next unsuspecting guy like he was a big catch in a fishing derby.

She took a big drink of her rum and Diet Coke, and then she squinted into the mirror and went back to adding more mascara onto her fake eyelashes.

Another sip of her drink, and another piece of advice: "Yep, a couple more weeks, and he'll be putty in my hands!" She laughed delightedly.

Then Clarice wriggled herself into the latest tight jumpsuit with extra wide bell-bottoms that she'd sewn for herself, shoved her feet into a pair of platform shoes, grabbed her cigarettes and her tiny little "clutch" covered in sequins and sparkles that she'd sewn onto a cheap bag she'd bought herself at Robertson's Department Store, and then she headed off in our "old beater" — a black 1962 Impala, with the tailpipe tied up with a bent-out coat hanger.

She gave a little wave out the window and yelled, "See ya later, Truly! Stay outta trouble now!"

That's my name, Truly Clarice Bateman. Apparently, my name was supposed to be Trudy, but when my birth certificate arrived it was discovered that my name had been accidentally recorded as Truly, and Clarice decided it was easier to just call me Truly than to go through all the hassle of the paperwork involved in getting it changed. So Truly it was. And that pretty much summed up Clarice's parenting style.

Don't get me wrong, I actually like it when Clarice is all excited about a new guy and is out every night trying to impress him. It's way better than when things don't work out for her. That's when she gets depressed, and even gets mean to me. She sleeps all day, and then gets up and moons around the trailer. She drinks a lot more on those days, calls in sick to work, and cries a lot, so I try to keep out of sight.

When things get really bad, I slip over to Andy El's trailer, and I know that I can sleep on the old green plaid couch on her covered back porch. She always seems to know when things are extra rough for me, and on those nights, she leaves a pillow and blanket out for me.

Andy El's nephew Raymond built the covered-in porch onto her trailer one fall. He showed up on a Friday after work with his old pickup truck loaded with some scrap plywood and two-by-fours from a construction site he was working on, and he spent a whole weekend hammering and sawing and made that porch a really nice place for Andy El. She moved an old fridge out there for extra storage.

A couple of months later, Raymond even came home with a salvaged window and an old door and added them. That's when Andy El dragged an old kitchen table and chairs and a green plaid couch out there. So now it stays pretty warm, even in the winter. It's nice and snug, and Andy El claims her trailer is even warmer than before.

Anyways, back to my lemonade stand. And my first ever customer, Elvis Presley. I just poured him a glass, trying to control my nervous hand, and then stood there and stared stupidly at him as he drank it down.

"Thanks," he said, dropping a dime onto the table. "Say, can you tell me where the office is?"

"Office?" I asked.

"The trailer park office," he said patiently.

"Oh, right," I said quickly. I pointed to Andy El's trailer. "There's no real office. You just need to talk to Andy El. You just go over to that blue and white trailer over there and knock on the door. Andy El's in the kitchen, or out in the yard doing some laundry, so just give a knock and then yell if she doesn't come right away."

He smiled at me, put the glass on the table, and said, I kid you not, "Thank you. Thank you very much."

He got back in that gold Sun Bug and drove over the bouncy ground to Andy El's. I just sat there, kind of stunned, and watched as he got out, knocked on the trailer door, and then chatted with Andy El. She handed him a set of keys and gestured to me to come over.

I left the stand and headed over to them, and she asked me to show Elvis the way to the empty green and white trailer with the “For Rent” sign in the little window beside the door.

“This way,” I said, and pointed to the trailer. It was all I could choke out. I mean, this was Elvis. Just what do you say to the King of Rock and Roll?

He followed me in his Sun Bug, bumping slowly over the rough ground.

I stood and gaped as he parked, got out and unlocked the trailer door, and started to unload his belongings from the car. I watched, mesmerized, as he unloaded two suitcases and a guitar case and took them into the trailer. Then he came back for three garment bags, carefully unhooking them from the hook behind the driver’s seat. One was a clear plastic dry-cleaning bag, and inside was a white jump-suit with a large, high collar and wide bell-bottoms. It was covered in sequins and looked just like an outfit Elvis Presley would have worn.

He draped it over his arm, and before he stepped inside the trailer, he turned to me, smiled, and said again, “Well, thank you. Thank you very much,” and then closed the door.

I stumbled back to the stand and sat down in stunned silence, realizing what this meant. Elvis Presley was renting the empty trailer at Eagle Shores. Ladies and gentlemen, Elvis was in the trailer park.

CHAPTER 2

Okay, I do realize that Elvis Presley has been dead for almost a year now, but that actually may not be true. I happen to be a bit of an expert on Elvis Presley. Up until a few months ago, Clarice had a good friend named Angela who worked at the tavern with her. Out of all of the friends who came and went out of Clarice's life, I really liked Angela. She actually paid attention to me and didn't make me feel like I was a pest or someone to be tolerated, the way the rest of Clarice's friends usually did.

Angela was a really big Elvis fan, and each week she bought every magazine going that featured a story on him. She would bring them over on Monday afternoons, since they both had that day off work. We have an old portable record player in the trailer, and she would go through Clarice's collection of older Elvis records and play them over and over.

I know Clarice doesn't really like Elvis that much, but she tolerated Angela's obsession because she brought us takeout fish and chips for dinner, and it was one meal a week that Clarice didn't have to think about cooking.

Angela would put on a record and dance around the trailer.

"This is an early recording," she'd say to me, "from his Sun Records days. Sam Phillips was such a fool to sell his contract off."

Then she'd shake her head at Clarice and say, "I don't understand why you don't play these records anymore, Clarice. You used to listen to Elvis all the time when we were in high school!"

And one day, as I sat on the floor looking at a magazine cover and listening to "Return to Sender," I overheard Clarice say to Angela in a bitter whisper, "Look, they aren't my records. They belonged to you-know-who. He was the one who played them all the time — I just put up with it. He was the world's biggest Elvis fan — even bigger than you. When he left, he left them behind, and that's all I have to remember him by — a bunch of Elvis records and, of course, Truly."

I pretended that I hadn't heard. I knew it had something to do with my mysterious dad, so I kept my head down, hoping she'd say more about him. But she didn't. So now I knew something about my father — he was an Elvis fan.

I read the magazines too, since Angela always left them behind and we didn't have any kid-type books hanging around the trailer. So I have become fairly knowledgeable about the King. I figured if my dad liked him that much, I should learn all that I could. The more I learned about Elvis, the more real my father became, and it felt good to have something in common with him.

And then, last year, when the announcement came that Elvis had died, it felt like the whole world just stopped. Angela really fell apart. You would have thought that Elvis was *her* boyfriend the way she cried and carried on. Even Clarice was shocked and upset by the big news that Elvis Presley had been found dead. He always seemed larger than life, so it was hard to believe.

I tried not to show it to Clarice, but I was pretty upset too. I imagined what my dad was feeling and wished that he could be there with us. He must have been so sad, too.

A couple of months after the death of Elvis, Angela decided that she was wasting her life working at the tavern, and she signed up to go to university. She announced she was moving away to Vancouver to go to some place called UBC. For some reason this made Clarice bitter and angry at Angela.

Angela stopped in to say goodbye to me on her way to

the ferry to Vancouver. We had one last quick dinner of fish and chips, and she slipped me an old postcard with her new address scrawled on it.

"This is where I'll be living from now on, Truly," she said. "Maybe when Clarice gets over being mad at me, the two of you can come over on the ferry and visit me for a weekend." She gave me a big hug and headed off. I watched her drive away, and felt sad. Just as sad as I felt when I heard that Elvis had died.

Clarice, meanwhile, went through the trailer, gathered up all of the magazines and the Elvis records, and threw them all in the trash.

And just like that, no more Elvis-filled Mondays with Angela, no more takeout fish and chips. No more feeling connected to my father. And another person was gone out of my life.

I waited until Clarice was at work later that day and picked some of Angela's magazines out of the garbage. The records were all broken and the covers were all bent up, so I had to let those go. I carefully cut out some of the articles about Elvis and hid them in an old shoebox in the closet.

Now, whenever I am in a grocery store with Clarice, I wait at the magazine rack until she's done all her shopping, and I read whatever news I can find on Elvis. It makes me feel a bit closer to Angela — and, of course, my father.

So this is how I happen to know that there is a distinct possibility that Elvis is alive and well and just trying to live out a normal life in peace and quiet somewhere. And now here he was, at the Eagle Shores Trailer Park. If only my dad knew that his hero was here!

After a few more hours of lemonade selling, I decided enough was enough. I couldn't stand just sitting there, watching the ice melt, all the while dying to know more about the new tenant. Besides, to my surprise, I had sold a few more glasses of lemonade, and the jug was now nearly empty.

I poured the last of the watery juice into a glass and drank it down, and then packed everything up. I took the jug and glasses to Andy El's trailer to wash, because I figured Clarice was either sewing or getting ready for work and wouldn't want me banging around getting in the way at our trailer. And this way, I could ask Andy El about the new tenant.

I knocked on the door, then just walked in, just like the rest of Andy El's family always does when they stop by.

Andy El was sitting at her gray Formica table in the little kitchenette drinking a mug of tea. The table and counters were filled with jars of newly-canned strawberry jam.

I filled the sink with soapy water and began washing the lemonade jug and glasses, and Andy El got out a small plate for me and put out a warm piece of fry bread, slathering it with fresh strawberry jam.

I joined her at the table and took a huge bite of the puffy fry bread. It was heaven. Andy El poured me a cup of tea with lots of milk in it, just how I liked it, and passed it over to me.

"So, was business good today?" she asked me. I grinned at her.

"It actually went okay," I said. "Took me a couple of hours, but I sold out." Andy El smiled and nodded, satisfied. She would never say "I told you so," but I could feel it there, sitting at the table with us.

"Mrs. Williams went out to town for groceries, and on her way back to her trailer she pulled up and had a glass. She told me it was a real treat, and I should keep it up all summer!" I couldn't help feeling proud, as though the whole stand idea had been mine.

"Well, that's just great!" said Andy El. "Good sign that you should keep it going, then! It'll give you something to do so you don't get bored, and you can earn a bit of money, too!"

Mrs. Williams was one of the first residents of the trailer park, and grew beautiful roses in her little garden on the sunny side of her trailer. She liked to bake, and would sometimes bring me some chocolate chip cookies or a loaf of raisin bread. She lived in the trailer next door to Clarice's and was always really nice to me — even when Clarice came home late at night and was loud coming into the trailer, singing or swearing as she stumbled around trying to open the trailer door.

"Where'd you get all the berries for the jam?" I asked Andy El. I knew strawberries were a luxury, and not something that Andy El would just go out and buy.

She smiled proudly at me.

"Raymond brought me five salmon last night when he came back from fishing out in the bay, so I walked over to Mrs. Wyman's this morning and offered to trade her a couple of them for some strawberries."

Mr. and Mrs. Wyman owned the farm down the road, between the four-way stop and the reserve land. They grew the best strawberries around, and everybody in town came to their you-pick or to buy from their fruit stand.

"I want you to walk over and take a couple of salmon to them, okay?" Andy El said to me as she passed me another piece of fry bread. Her timing was so good there was no way I could say no to her. "I got them all cleaned and wrapped."

I sighed, said, "Okay," and then bit into the warm, golden fry bread.

Andy El said, "Well, Mr. Wyman's dog had some puppies. You know, they have that lab called Lady? I saw them pups in the barn when I went strawberry picking. Maybe today when you go over you can take a look at them. Pretty cute pups."

I finished my fry bread and licked the jam off my hands. Then Andy El gave me the two salmon wrapped up in newspaper.

I headed for the door, but then I stopped and turned back. I had to ask her about Elvis.

"Um … Andy El?" I asked. "So that new tenant, the guy who rented the trailer today — do you know who he is?"

"Well, of course I do," she replied. She got up and peered at the lease papers she'd had him sign, which she'd left on the counter by the phone. "Says here his name is Aaron Kingsley. He'll be renting for the summer, for three months at least. Maybe even longer, he says."

"Andy El, don't you think he looks like — Elvis?" I asked her. "You know, Elvis Presley?" Andy El just looked surprised. "Elvis Presley?" she said. "That singer fella?" I nodded eagerly.

"Well, that's just silly. That fella died, didn't he? Last summer sometime? And what the heck would he be doing here, if he was alive, at my little trailer park?" She chuckled, poured herself some more tea, and then said, "You get that salmon over to Mrs. Wyman, and make sure you see those pups. They sure are cute!"

I picked up the damp salmon and scuffed my way down the dusty road to the Wymans' farm. They had a farm stand on the road and sold eggs, produce, strawberries, and lots more. I turned down the driveway and checked that Mr. Wyman's truck was in the driveway beside the house.

I peeked inside the barn and said a nervous "Hello?" to the dark interior. As my eyes adjusted to the gloom, I could see a big worktable that was covered in baskets of strawberries. No one was there.

Just then, I heard someone walking up from the field behind the barn, so I turned and politely waited as Mrs. Wyman came into view carrying two more baskets of freshly picked strawberries.

"Why, hello there," she said to me. "You're Clarice's girl, Truly, aren't you?"

"Yes, ma'am," I said. "Andy El asked me to bring over some salmon for you."

I handed her the wrapped fish, and she said, "Well, you tell her thanks again, will you? This will be a real treat!"

She turned to take the salmon into the house, and I said, "Um … Mrs. Wyman? Andy El told me your dog had puppies. May I see them? If it's not too much trouble?"

"Well, sure! Come and take a look! They're over here," she said kindly. She put the salmon down on the table beside the strawberries and led the way over to the furthest corner of the barn, to a pile of old quilts on a bed of straw. There was Lady, the Wymans' lab, snuggled up with the cutest squiggling mass of puppies I had ever seen.

"Oh ..." I breathed. "They're so cute!"

"Go ahead, pick one up," she said. I stepped closer and let Lady sniff my hand to get to know me. She gave me a lick, so I figured she was letting me know that it was okay for me to pick up one of the pups.

"Here, Truly," said Mrs. Wyman, "you can hold one," and she reached in to the mass of wriggling little bodies and picked up a small brown puppy with white socks on his front feet. She handed him carefully to me.

"Ohhh, wow," I said. He licked my nose, and then yawned. He had a glorious smell, a blend of straw and puppy. I grinned down at him.

"What kind are they?" I asked.

"Well now, Lady is a purebred lab, but we aren't really sure just what the father was." I snuggled the pup carefully.

"Hello there," I said to him. He washed my face and wriggled in my arms, but I held him firmly so he wouldn't fall.

"You and me are a lot alike," I said to him. "Nobody knows who my dad is either."

I smiled down at him and gave him a kiss on the top of his head. When I looked up at Mrs. Wyman she had a sort of funny look on her face and was wiping her eye, like she had something in it. Maybe a piece of straw or some farm dust.

I put the puppy carefully back with the seven others and watched, grinning, as they tumbled and scrambled around and over each other. After a few moments I figured I'd better go, since I didn't want to be a pest and keep Mrs. Wyman from her farm work. I wanted to make sure that I would be welcome back to see these puppies another day.

So I reluctantly dragged myself away and asked, "What will you do with all the puppies?"

"Well, I guess we'll put them up for sale when they're old enough to leave Lady," said Mrs. Wyman. "We may keep one, but we certainly can't keep all eight of them!"

"Thanks again for letting me see them," I said and headed back to the trailer park.

CHAPTER 3

When I got back to the trailer park, I headed down to our trailer, since I could hear the stereo blaring some god-awful disco tune. That meant Clarice was up and hopefully in a fairly decent mood.

I opened the door, stepped in, and yelled "Hi, Clarice!" to let her know that I was home. I looked around at the trailer and saw sequins and shiny fabric everywhere — on the table, on the couch — with pattern pieces spread out on the worn carpet in our little living room. There was no place for me to stand, much less sit.

"Hey, Truly, whatcha been doin'?" she called absently from the bathroom. I looked in and found her putting on her makeup. Her blush, eyeshadow, and makeup brushes were littered all around the edges of the sink.

"I'm headin' out to work pretty soon, kid," she said, "so don't mess up my sewing stuff. I been workin' all day on these things. I got the patterns all sized and cut out, and have everything where I need it to get started on the sewing tomorrow. I got a day off tomorrow, and Byron's outta town, so I'm gonna sew all day."

Clarice worked nights at the Newman Bay Hotel and Tavern, and took in the odd sewing job to "make ends meet." Not that any ends meet too often in our place. I spend a lot of time on my own, while Clarice goes her own way. She spends a lot of time sewing on her old Brother sewing machine if she isn't working or out on dates with the next Mr. Wrong.

Believe it or not, Clarice is good at sewing. She could remodel an old outfit and turn it into something really flashy, just like you'd see in a magazine. She just loves poring over magazines looking at disco outfits, and then she heads out to a local thrift shop to buy fabric or old dresses and stuff. She hunkers down over the sewing machine and remakes her finds into some spectacular outfits for herself.

Clarice also takes in paid sewing jobs. She's always hemming skirts and jeans and doing alterations for people from town for extra money. But there's one important thing that everyone in town either knows or has learned the hard way: absolutely do not bring her a sewing job at the end of the week.

That's when she starts her serious drinking, and the quality of her work goes right downhill. The rule of thumb is, no later than a Wednesday, Thursday morning if it's a quick job, like hemming a skirt. Because by Thursday late afternoon, the quality of her sewing is dropping, and by Friday it is downright disastrous. One time on a Friday, she hemmed the same pant leg twice for the high school principal's wife, and the woman was as mad as a wet hen. And that made Clarice just as furious, because she had to pay out the money for a whole new pair of pants to replace them. I stayed clear of the trailer for two days until she calmed down that time.

Usually if Clarice is home, she is mooning around, chain-smoking and listening to the radio while she sews. Like I say, she's good at sewing, but she can get cranky while she hunches over her sewing machine, so I learned early to be real quiet or just get out of the trailer when she had a big job to do.

As of this week, she is working on the new majorette costumes for the Newman Bay High Steppers majorette troupe. It's a very big job.

My grandmother, Clarice's mom, runs the majorette troupe for the town. In fact, she started the whole High Steppers majorette troupe years ago. Clarice used to be the head majorette when she was much younger, proudly marching down Main Street in the parade every year. That was before she had me, of course.

My grandmother was Mrs. Bateman, who owns a little

corner grocery store on the outskirts of town and lives above it in a small, cramped apartment. That's where she'd raised Clarice until Clarice "ruined her life" by having a child at such a young age. To the end of her days, Mrs. Bateman would never get over the mortification of having her only child have to leave school in grade ten, when she'd had such a bright future ahead of her.

We would only visit Mrs. Bateman occasionally, and would sit carefully on the edge of her plastic-covered couch, after wading our way through boxes of batons and majorette hats. Usually this was when Clarice really ran short of money, and even she noticed the lack of food in the trailer and was then forced to borrow money from the "old battle-axe," as she called her mother. Behind her back, of course.

Me, I just always called her Mrs. Bateman. To her face and behind her back. I knew she didn't like me much, and she always seemed to be bitterly angry with Clarice. She was thin and pinched and mean-looking. It never occurred to any of us that I should call her "Granny" or "Grandmother."

She was always very proud to tell us that she still managed to run that store six days a week, Monday to Saturday. Still respected the Lord's Day and closed on Sundays, *and* got the High Steppers to the island finals each year, once even bringing home the championship and the big trophy. According to her, that's why the Town Council and the

Chamber of Commerce didn't vote to have her quit running the majorette troupe after the Big Scandal. Because she could still take a group of eager young girls and mold them into a precision machine of glorious twirling, marching majorettes that made this town proud.

And it was a relief to her that she could still hold her head up high in this town and that parents would still trust her with their young daughters after her own had chosen to defy her and ruin her life in such a shameful way.

Thank the lord Clarice still had a way with sequins and could come up with a new costume every few years for the troupe. According to Mrs. Bateman, it was Clarice's only saving grace.

So, needless to say, we didn't see Mrs. Bateman too much. Only when Clarice was really short on cash or we had to pick up or drop off majorette costumes needing repairs.

This year, the summer of 1978, according to Mrs. Bateman, the High Steppers had a real good shot again at the island championship with their new top-secret routine, and she had managed to convince the Chamber of Commerce that the girls needed some fancy new uniforms to help clinch their victory.

So now Clarice was under pressure to get them all designed, fitted, and sewn by the July fifteenth parade down Main Street. That was when the town held Newman

Bay Days, a weekend-long festival to celebrate the founding of the town. On the Saturday morning there was always a pancake breakfast followed by the big parade. This would be the troupe's big chance to sashay down through town and show off to the cheering crowd the slick new routines they would take to the championship, held near the end of August, up island in Nanaimo.

I was actually kind of relieved now to have the lemonade stand to run, so I had something to do that would keep me out of the trailer till the costumes were all done. Maybe Andy El was right about that.

Clarice hated getting up early, but she knew she had to if she was going to get all the costumes finished in time. And these new ones were going to be loaded to the gills with sequins, judging by the state of our trailer.

"You can find something in the fridge and make yourself some dinner, but stay outta the living room! Bye kid!" she yelled as she headed out the door.

I sighed and crunched carefully through all of the scattered sequin strands to turn off the radio that she had left blaring.

I headed to the kitchenette, opened the fridge, and dug around. I found a couple of hot dogs. On the counter were some buns that were a bit dry, but would still be okay. I put the wieners in a pot of water to boil and found some mustard to put on the buns. When the wieners were ready, I lifted them out carefully with a fork and laid them on the buns. I carried them in my hands so I didn't dirty a plate and went out to the trailer step and sat to eat.

When I finished eating, I went back inside and washed the pot and fork. That wasn't so much because I was a tidy kid, it was more in self-defense — this way Clarice had nothing extra to be mad at me about. When I threw the empty hot dog bun bag in the garbage, I noticed a crumpled-up postcard, where Clarice had tossed it. I pulled it out and smoothed it flat on the counter. On the front was a picture of one of the B.C. ferries. I flipped it over and saw that it was from Angela. The writing was small and cramped, so she could fit it all in.

So I made it here! I'm staying with my aunt near Stanley Park while I go to school.

Guess who I saw in Kitsilano the other day? You-know-who! Truly sure looks like him! You really do need to tell him about her. He's working at a restaurant here. Come over and visit for a weekend and bring Truly! Say hi to her for me, miss you both, Angela.

My mind was whirling and my heart was pounding in my chest. Just like that, Angela had found my dad.

I got myself a glass of cold tap water and then just sat outside on the grass, sipping it slowly to help my stomach feel full, and thought over everything Angela had written.

She had seen my dad! She'd even invited us over to go meet with him. He was just a ferry ride away, somewhere in Vancouver, and Angela knew just where to find him. My heart was pounding. I could finally meet him.

I had never been on the ferry, but everybody knows that you can catch the bus at the stop on the highway, and it takes you straight out to the ferry terminal.

Then, I knew from listening to Angela trying to convince Clarice to come and visit her for a weekend, you just buy another bus ticket on the ferry, and when the ferry docks, you walk down to the car deck and climb onto the bus. It takes you all the way downtown to the Vancouver bus terminal. From there, I knew that I could ask what bus would take me to Stanley Park, and from there, I could just ask directions to get myself to Angela's address.

I also knew Clarice would never take me to meet my father. But if I had the money, I could go on my own. If I kept the lemonade stand going, I could save up the money that I earned. When I had enough saved, I could just pick a weekend and go to Vancouver. I could walk to the bus stop on the highway, I reasoned, take the bus to the ferry, and get on the ferry to Vancouver. And then I could stay with Angela. She would take me to meet my dad. That way I could tell him all about Elvis, how he was now living at the trailer park. My father needed to know that. He must still be so sad about Elvis dying, and this would make him so happy. He might even come back home to live with Clarice and me, to be near Elvis.

As I sat, I barely noticed that the sun was setting and dusk was setting in. I knew that I needed to keep this a secret. I couldn't tell anyone about my plan to go to Vancouver. It would be best to keep that to myself until the day that I went.

Then I could just leave a note saying that I was going to visit Angela, and it would be too late for Clarice to stop me meeting my dad.

As the sun went down, it began to get a bit chilly. I shivered and thought about the puppies I had seen at the Wymans' farm, and how nice it would be to have one of those puppies. But I knew that was something that could never happen. There was no way that Clarice would agree to me having a dog.

I wondered if my dad would have let me get a dog, if he were around. Then I started to imagine what it would be like to have my dad living here at the trailer. And a puppy. Like a real family.

And that's when I decided that if anyone asked me what

I was saving my money for, I would just say it was to buy one of the puppies. I needed a good cover story, in case anyone asked me.

I hung around the trailer making my plans till it got real dark, and then I slipped over to Andy El's trailer to sleep on her porch.

CHAPTER 4

The next morning, I was up early in Andy El's kitchen, making the lemonade and getting the glasses out to the stand. I took the metal ice cube tray to the kitchen sink and pried loose the cubes. I dumped them into the lemonade jug, refilled the tray, and replaced it in the small freezer in the fridge.

Andy El sat watching me, having her morning tea at the kitchen table. I sat down at the table across from her.

"Andy El?" I asked hesitantly. "How much does it cost to get a dog? Do you think I could earn enough with the lemonade stand to get a dog by the end of the summer?"

She looked at me in surprise.

"Well, now," she said finally. "You talk to Clarice about that? What does she think of that idea?"

"I haven't talked to her about it," I confessed. "I just think it would be so nice to have a dog. You know, he'd be waiting when I get home from school, all excited to see me, and I could walk him, and feed him, and take care of him ..." I trailed off. I knew in my heart Clarice would never go for a puppy, and I started to feel awful not telling Andy El the truth about why I really wanted to save up the lemonade stand money.

Finally, Andy El said thoughtfully, "Maybe we can put out a few jars of my jam to sell — you just never know! We can sell 'em for fifty cents, and you can keep twenty-five cents from each jar you sell."

I looked up at her in surprise. I knew that the jam she had made was meant to last through the whole winter, and that she always gave whatever extra jars she had to her family members. Andy El's family always helped each other out and shared whatever they had. And giving me jars to sell at the stand meant that there wouldn't be as much jam to go around. Strawberry jam was a real treat for all of them, and here was Andy El, just giving it away to me to sell.

Wordlessly, I went over to Andy El and gave her a huge hug, and just held on tight to her. She stroked my hair and held me tight too. Then she got up and bustled around, making more tea and getting me a piece of fry bread. I wanted to tell her what I was really saving the money for, but I knew that I couldn't. I knew Andy El wouldn't like me going on the ferry by myself, and she would find a way to stop me.

"You go on over this afternoon and see those pups again, and ask Mr. Wyman how much he wants for one."

I just stood staring at Andy El. I could barely trust that this was happening. I was going to meet my dad. And tell him about Elvis. He would come home, and maybe he would let me have a puppy.

"Oh, Andy El," I whispered. "Do you think it could really happen?" She just grinned at me, handed me the piece of fry bread, and then passed the jar of jam. Of course, she thought I was talking about getting a dog. *But maybe I can*, I thought to myself, *if my dad comes back*.

"You betcha!" she said. "We could use a good dog around here!"

Then she said, "You can have five jars to sell to start with."

I ate as fast as I could, jumped up, and rinsed my plate. Then I got to work making a new sign for the table that read: *Lemonade Stand 10 cents a glass. Homemade Strawberry Jam 50 cents.*

It was official. I was in business and earning money. I felt really bad about not telling Andy El the truth about what I was going to save my money for, but when my dad came back with me from Vancouver, I was really sure that he would agree to get me a dog. So it wasn't really a lie, I reasoned. I headed out to set up my stand.

I was pretty jittery all day at the stand. It felt like the longest day ever, as I waited between customers for the opportunity to come for me to close up for the day and then walk over to the Wymans' farm to ask about the puppies. At the end of the summer, I reasoned, if it didn't work out with my dad to get a puppy, that would be okay. Because the puppy was just a cover story anyway.

Word was getting out about my stand, and several of the other trailer park residents stopped in for a glass.

Mrs. Marshall, the retired teacher who had a double-wide right below Andy El's trailer with a real fine view of the bay, stopped in on her way back from the mailbox out at the road.

"Oh, my, this is a nice treat," she said. "Mrs. Williams told me all about this."

She sipped at her glass and asked me how things were going.

"Fine," I said.

"How was school this year?" she persisted.

"It was okay," I answered. I liked to be noncommittal, especially with my new lemonade stand customers. I wasn't going to tell her that I had simply suffered through this year as I did every year at school. That I had spent my days feeling like an outsider, having to once again show up with used notebooks from previous years, and most days with little or no lunch. That I had spent my lunchtimes and recesses alone, sitting in the library or out under the huge old oak tree watching everyone else shriek and laugh with their friends.

I wasn't going to tell her how the other kids had years before finally given up trying to get me to hang out or talk, because they all knew that I was Clarice's kid, and that meant I wasn't really good friend material. Sure, one or two had taken pity on me and invited me to their homes to hang out after school, but we all knew that I couldn't do the same in return. So I always made some excuse and turned them down. They always seemed relieved. I know I was when they went back to leaving me alone.

Mrs. Marshall finished her glass and put it down on the table, saying, "Well, this is a real nice treat for all of us here at the park, Truly. Will you be here every day?"

"I think so," I said casually. "I'll see how the summer goes, I guess."

I didn't want to mention my puppy plan to anyone until I had talked to the Wymans. And I sure didn't want to mention that I was really saving to go and meet my dad. If I asked the Wymans about possibly buying a puppy, that would help my cover story, I figured.

Mrs. Marshall smiled encouragingly at me and said, "Well, you can count on me to be here every day!" and she took her mail back to her trailer. I had another regular customer!

About an hour later, Elvis stepped out of his trailer and walked over to the stand.

And once again, I just sat there staring like an idiot at him as he approached me.

"Howdy," he said with a smile. He took off his aviator sunglasses and said, "I'll take a glass of that lemonade. Sure is good!" I managed to pour him a glass without spilling too much in my nervousness, and handed it to him.

"Thanks," he said. "So, your name is Truly, is that right?"

"Yup, Truly Clarice Bateman. That's me." I flushed as I realized how foolish I must have sounded, telling him my entire name like that. Like I wanted him to sign an autograph or something.

He grinned at me. "TCB. Nice initials," he said.

Desperately searching for something to say to him as he drank his lemonade, I finally blurted out, "So, you're a musician?" and then I added lamely, "Um … I saw you take a guitar into your trailer."

He smiled at me, took a sip, squinted out at the view of the bay, and finally said, "Well, yes I am. At least I was, once. I was pretty good, too. A few years back I got pretty well-known, too."

"Oh," I said. Not sterling conversation, but it was all I could come up with for a reply.

Then he grinned again at me, put his empty glass down, and said, "Well, you never know, I might just be real famous again one day."

Then he asked me for directions to town and recommendations for a good place to buy groceries.

I stumbled and stammered like an idiot through my explanation of how to get to town and the best grocery store to shop at. I sent him to the Newman Bay Food Mart. Andy El always said they have the best prices in town. Esther said that she preferred to shop there because the Chinese couple who owned it were very friendly, and they didn't seem to mind Indians coming in and shopping, not like some other stores in Newman Bay.

Esther once told me very bitterly that in some stores in town they were all treated very badly. For example, the clerks in Robertson's Department Store would always follow her around, glaring suspiciously at her like she was going to steal something. Robertson's was the only department store in the small town of Newman Bay, and that meant it was the only place where you could buy certain items, like a pair of jeans or running shoes, and other things that the dry goods store and the five-and-dime didn't carry.

So, while Esther and the other Natives from the Eagle Shores reserve would shop elsewhere whenever they could, it was hard to avoid Robertson's completely. Unless, of course, you had a car and could drive down to Victoria, which was about forty-five minutes away, and well over an hour and a half each way if you took the bus.

It was a bitter pill to swallow, Esther said, to have to go in and spend hard-earned money at a place like Robertson's, where even the manager would follow along while Esther looked through the racks of clothes for her girls, as though he was just waiting for the chance to catch her trying to rob them blind. All just because she was an Indian.

But I didn't mention all of that to Elvis. I didn't feel it was pertinent to his situation.

Besides, I was still stammering like a giddy Elvis fan whenever he was around.

Late in the afternoon I closed up the stand, washed the jug and glasses at Andy El's, and set them to dry in the dish rack. I decided to head on over to talk to the Wymans about a puppy. Andy El was out in the backyard hanging laundry on the line, so I told her where I was going and headed off before I chickened out.

I was so nervous as I approached the farm that I could feel my heart pounding away in my chest.

I took a deep breath and peeked into the barn. Mrs. Wyman was there, sorting strawberries into pint baskets and loading them into one of the three fridges kept in the barn for produce.

"Hello, Mrs. Wyman," I said nervously.

"Well, hello, Truly," she said, smiling. "Did you come to see the puppies again?"

I nodded, and she said, "Well, I could use a break from all these berries, so I'll join you."

We approached the puppies and knelt down in the straw beside them. Again I let Lady sniff my hand, and then gave her a pat on the head to let her know I was a friend. The little brown puppy came scrambling over to me, and to my delight he clambered right into my lap. I gave him a snuggle, and he settled right in.

Mrs. Wyman knelt down beside me and began to pat two puppies who were tumbling and playing in front of her.

"They sure are cute," I said.

She laughed as they fell over in a tangle. "They sure are, Truly."

I took a deep breath and said, "Mrs. Wyman, how much do you think you will sell them for? I've been doing really well so far with my lemonade stand, and I thought that I could save up all my money that I earn for one of the puppies. If they're not too expensive." It all came out in a rush.

"I'll work really hard all summer, and save all my money, and I promise to be a really responsible dog owner. I'll walk him every day, and feed him, and take real good care of him. I promise. I just think it would be so nice to have a dog …" I trailed away, worried that I had said too much and sounded like a babbling idiot. I ducked my head down and kept on petting the puppy, who had snuggled down on my lap. I was getting really carried away with my cover story. I knew in my heart that it wasn't really true. I wasn't really going to save money for a puppy, but it was hard to keep focused with that cute, puppy in my arms.

"Well, good heavens!" she said. "I don't know as we've set a price as yet. But I think Mr. Wyman was figuring about twenty dollars each."

I just stared at her wordlessly, my courage draining away. Twenty dollars. That was a lot of money. On top of the money I would need to get to Vancouver. Then I would have a leash and a collar to buy, and then dog food every week, too. My heart sank, but then that puppy licked my face as if to say, *It will all work out*, so I just sat and looked at her in hopeless silence.

"Well, dear, how much do you think you can raise from your lemonade stand?"

"I've made one dollar and seventy cents so far," I said proudly. "I still have to pay Andy El for the lemonade, of course, but after that, I figure I made about a dollar and thirty-five cents. Oh! I almost forgot! Andy El gave me some of her strawberry jam to sell at the stand too, and I get to keep twenty-five cents from every jar!"

Mrs. Wyman smiled so kindly at me that I started to feel a bit hopeful again.

"I think we can say that this particular puppy is on hold

for you, Truly," she said. "He sure seems to like you. You come over and visit him every few days, and let me know how much you've saved, and we will work out a fair price for you. He won't be ready to leave his mother till the end of the summer anyway, so you have lots of time to decide."

I gave the pup another kiss on the top of his head and put him back gently. "I'll be back soon, I promise!" I told him, but he was already hunkering down for a snooze with all the others.

"Thanks, Mrs. Wyman! I promise I'll earn all the money! And I'll be a real good dog owner! I'll take real good care of him. I'll walk him and feed him and brush him everyday!" I said as we headed back to the yard. I had nearly convinced myself that I was really going to get that puppy.

"I'm sure you will, Truly," said Mrs. Wyman. I waved to her and headed back to Eagle Shores. I wanted to tell Andy El all about the puppy.

"Just a minute, Truly," called Mrs. Wyman after me. "I'd like you to give these to Andy El for me." She held out two large baskets of the freshly picked strawberries.

"These ones are getting over-ripe so I can't put them out for sale, and I know she'll need some more for making jam."

She loaded me up with the baskets, and added, "You tell Andy El that if Raymond goes out fishing again and has some more extra salmon, I'll be happy to make another trade."

"Thanks, Mrs. Wyman!" I called and headed off back to the trailer park to tell Andy El the good news. And now she could make some more jam to give to her family and make up for the jars she had given me to sell at the table.

As I walked back to the reserve, I reflected on how much fun it had been to pretend, just for a few moments, while I held that cute puppy, that I really could buy him. Even though I knew that it wouldn't really happen.

Maybe Andy El is right, I thought to myself. *It is good to earn your own money, and you can dream about all the great stuff you can buy with it.*

CHAPTER 5

The next day, I got up early, made the first jug of lemonade, and filled it with ice by nine o'clock.

"I can pay you for the first six cans, now, Andy El! But I'm gonna need to buy some more real soon at this rate!" I proudly told her.

"That's okay, Truly, I got a lot more cans in the freezer out in the shed." She grinned at me. "I knew you'd need more, and I didn't want to bother Raymond with another ride to town so soon after the last run, so I bought lots for you."

Raymond was one of the only family members to have a vehicle and he could drive Andy El for groceries and such, when he wasn't busy working. He had a pretty good job, working for a construction company, doing cleanup and stuff on the job sites. Raymond was hardworking and very kind. He was always thinking of little things that he could do for Andy El and the rest of his family, doing repairs on houses, or driving them places in his pickup truck.

He was Andy El's youngest nephew, and was lots of fun. Andy El always called him her son, and he always called her Mama. He had a different last name from Andy El, which was very confusing to me, until I once asked Andy El about it when I heard someone call him Raymond Joseph.

"How come your son Raymond has a different last name from you?" I asked. I think I was about eight at the time, otherwise I don't think I would have been so brash.

She smiled at me and explained: "Well, Raymond is my late sister's son. She passed away, oh, long time ago now. See, in our tradition, Raymond is like a son to me, being my nephew. Now that his own mama has gone on, he has become even more my son. That's our way."

I thought about that for a long time, and how nice it would be to have your family care about you that much.

Raymond lived on the reserve proper, along with Andy El's grown-up kids. It was accessed through what was known as the Cut, which was just a short trail that had been cut years ago through a line of tall, sweeping cedar trees t hat ran from the side of the trailer park next to Andy El's trailer straight on down near the water.

Andy El had lots of grown kids: six boys, most of whom were off logging for most of the year and came home in winter-time, and three daughters too.

Esther was my favorite of her daughters. She was married

and had three kids, and she worked in a coffee shop in town. She was always laughing and she spent as much time with her twin daughters as she could when she wasn't working. They'd go off berry picking or digging for clams, and then bring part of whatever they harvested for Andy El. Her son was eighteen, and this summer he was off fishing for the whole summer on a commercial fishing boat, with his dad, Edgar. They were all real proud of him for becoming a commercial fisherman, like his dad. Her daughters were my age, as far as I knew.

I couldn't help feeling a bit jealous of those twin girls, Agnes and Linda. Clarice never seemed to want to spend time with me, and when she was home, I usually just tiptoed around her and tried to stay out of her way.

Today, my first customer was Mrs. Williams, who stopped by when she was walking back from the mailbox with her mail.

"Oh my, Andy El's homemade strawberry jam!" she said, digging into her purse for a dollar bill. "I'd better get some before it all sells out."

I gave her two jars and took the money, putting the dollar into my money jar.

"Whatever are you going to do with all of the money you make this summer?" she asked me. I liked Mrs. Williams a lot. Her husband had worked for years on the ferry, loading cars on and off the car deck. They had retired to live out their days in the trailer park, but Mr. Williams had died only a year or two after they'd moved in. That was years ago, way before Clarice and I had moved in, of course. Mrs. Williams had stayed on, planting all those beautiful rosebushes around her trailer.

I figured I could tell her about the puppy, because I knew she never spoke to Clarice much and wouldn't give me away. "Well, I'm hoping that I'll get enough money to get a dog," I said. "One of the Wymans' puppies."

"My, that's a big undertaking," she said, "but it would be lovely to have a dog around the trailer park. I think that's a grand idea!"

She finished her lemonade, began to walk away from the table, and headed off to her trailer.

She was back in a few minutes, carrying a handful of dog-eared paperback books.

"You know, dear, I had a thought. Why don't we put out some of my old books and see if they sell? You could price them at, say, five cents a book. And you can keep the profit. I was just going to get rid of them, anyway."

She looked so pleased with herself for her big idea that I didn't want to be rude, so I said, "Gee, what a great idea!" like I really meant it.

I shuffled things around to fit the books in with the

lemonade and jars of jam and made a new sign saying: *Books for Sale, 5 cents.* I sighed. *Some lemonade stand*, I thought. *It's starting to look more like a rummage sale table now!*

With another big sigh, I picked up one of Mrs.Williams's books. It was a mystery about an old lady named Miss Marple, who lived in a small town in England and solved crimes. And she did it just by watching and listening to the people around her. I really got into it, and it helped pass the time between lemonade customers.

I really liked the book. I could see where I had a lot in common with the main character. Okay, so I'm eleven and not an old lady, but I do sit quietly and watch people, just like her. Only for Miss Marple it was out of a keen sense of interest. She wasn't really being nosy; she was just terribly interested in people.

In my case, I was just trying to gauge whether or not I should stay out of Clarice's way, as well as all her boyfriends who came and went. I needed to know when to hightail it out of our trailer and get over to the safety of Andy El's back porch, for instance, and when the coast was clear to go back home to our trailer.

I had read nearly half the book by the time Andy El called me in for lunch, and then we mixed up another jug of lemonade. She gave me a few more jars of jam to put out on the stand, since they had proved to be a big seller. I was just putting them out on the table when Elvis showed up for a glass of lemonade.

"Well, hello there, Truly," he said to me, smiling that famous smile. Just like in one of his movies.

"Hello, Mr. Kingsley," I said. It came out as barely a whisper, but at least I got something out of my mouth this time. As I poured him a glass of lemonade, he checked out the other things for sale on my table.

"Well, now, homemade strawberry jam. That's a real favorite of mine," he said. Then, I swear, he leaned over and whispered, as though to keep anyone from hearing him, "I have a real weakness for peanut butter sandwiches, and nothin' goes better than strawberry jam on them!"

I sat there, just gaping like a guppy, as he fished out a dollar and handed it to me, then took two jars of jam.

That sealed it! Everybody knew that Elvis had a weakness for peanut butter! All the magazines said so, and he'd just admitted to it!

As he drove off in his Bug, I was hit with a brilliant plan. I could use all of my detecting skills to keep an eye on him and prove that it really was Elvis Presley living in our trailer park. Just like that Miss Marple did in the book. Then I would have some hard facts to tell my dad. And then he would really want to come home.

After lunch, Mr. Wyman drove past his own farm gate to stop in at my stand for a glass of lemonade. "Heard about this here stand," he said cheerfully. "Can't resist a good glass of lemonade." He wiped his brow with his blue bandana and then stuffed it back in his pocket.

"Say," he said. "Agatha Christie books, eh? Better pick up a couple for the missus." He took four of the books and gave me a quarter, saying, "Keep the change, Truly. Oh, I hear you're going to buy one of our puppies! That's just great. You make sure you stop by and visit your dog anytime!"

"Thanks, Mr. Wyman," I said. I was elated.

I actually started to think that maybe this stand was going to be an okay way to spend the summer. I was going to go to Vancouver, find my dad, and tell him that Elvis was still alive and living at Eagle Shores. And maybe I'd get that dog, after all. Maybe something good would come my way for once.

CHAPTER 6

Lemonade sales seemed to get steady after that, and by the end of the day I had sold out two whole jugs of lemonade, two more books, and three more jars of jam.

My money jar was getting pretty full. When I packed up at the end of the day, I carefully wrote a tally of how much of the money was Andy El's for jam, and how much was mine. So far, I had made $2.75!

I was pretty excited. I stopped in at Andy El's to tell her how great we were doing and to leave my jar of money with her for safe keeping.

She looked at me and said, "It's really important to know how to earn some money and how to save it carefully, Truly. Some people have a really hard time with that. This'll be a really good summer for you to learn this. And it's a fun way to earn some money, too."

She gave me a big hug and told me she was really proud of me. I felt proud of me, too. I almost let myself believe that something good could happen to me. I nearly blurted out my whole plan about going to find my dad, but I stopped myself.

I headed back to my trailer to check in with Clarice and see how the costumes were going.

She had the radio cranked and was singing along as she sewed, hunched over the sewing machine and muttering every few minutes about seeing sequins in her sleep.

"Hey, Clarice," I said, trying to assess her mood. How long I hung around the trailer when Clarice was home was always dependent on what her mood was.

"What you been doing, Truly?" she asked through a mouthful of pins.

"Not much," I said. "Just thought I'd get something to eat. You hungry?"

"Nah, I can grab something to eat later at work," she said, concentrating on her sewing. A moment later she added, "Whatcha been doing? You stayin' outta trouble?"

I was reluctant to tell her about the lemonade stand, even though I knew she'd find out sooner or later. I knew that she'd take all of the fun out of it when she did find out. Usually she'd laugh at anything I tried to do.

Clarice is not terribly maternal. That's what Esther and Andy El said, one Saturday morning when I was about six, after Clarice had packed up all my favorite toys and my beloved doll and sold them for extra money at the flea market at the local community hall.

"What are you cryin' about?" Clarice had yelled at me. "At least they aren't cluttering up the joint anymore, and at least I got enough cash for some hot dogs and a pack of smokes out of it!"

Broken-hearted, I had simply turned away and run straight to Andy El's trailer, where I found her sitting with Esther, having tea at the kitchen table. I climbed up on Andy El's lap, snuffling and hiccupping, and told her what Clarice had done. She just held me and rocked me as I sobbed in her arms till I fell asleep.

Later, I woke up in Andy El's living room on the couch, where she had laid me down to nap with a crocheted blanket over me.

Snuggled next to me was a much-loved old doll with a faded blue dress.

Andy El sat down next to me, again pulled me onto her lap, and explained that while Clarice was doing her best, she just didn't know enough to be a good mother. Then she and Esther introduced me to Pattycake, Esther's old doll that Andy El still kept.

"I want you to look after her for me, Truly," Esther said, very seriously, as she placed the doll on my lap. "These days she just stays here with Andy El, but she gets too busy to watch out for Pattycake. So I want you to do it for me, will you promise?"

I just held on to that old doll real tight and, with big eyes, nodded a wordless promise to Esther and Andy El.

I lay back down again on the couch with Pattycake, singing her a song quietly and stroking her black hair gently so she wouldn't be scared of me, and I heard Esther say to Andy El, "Honestly, Mama, that woman doesn't have a maternal bone in her body. How could anyone do that to a child!"

Andy El whispered, "You hush now, I don't want Truly to hear that." But I had. And I covered Pattycake's ears so she wouldn't hear them talking about Clarice.

It took me a few more years to learn exactly what having a maternal bone meant, but by the time I did learn the meaning of the word *maternal*, I had been living so long as Clarice's cast-off daughter that I realized that I really did understand it, right down to the marrow of my own bones.

I still looked out for Pattycake and kept her safe at Andy El's, even though I knew that I was way too big for dolls.

In fact, Pattycake still slept in Andy El's living room in a place of honor beside her knitting basket, in a little wooden doll bed that Raymond had made as a surprise for my seventh birthday. She was still covered in the little patchwork doll blanket that Andy El had made her out of some old dresses she had. I knew she was loved and had a safe place there at Andy El's trailer. Me and Pattycake had that in common.

I still hadn't told Clarice about my dog plan. Even though it wasn't my real plan, I was very reluctant to tell her. I knew that she would shoot the idea down. And laugh at me. She'd sit back, slap her knee, and give a real belly laugh that would turn into a jeer. And then she would say something like, "No freakin' way" to me getting a dog.

I would love to have a puppy, but I knew there was no way I could. Clarice could barely look after me, so I knew that there was no way we could have a dog and look after it properly. And really, it was just my cover story. I sure couldn't tell her about my real plan — to go on the ferry by myself to visit Angela and convince her to take me to meet my dad. If I could tell him that Elvis was now living at the trailer park, I knew he'd want to come back to us.

Also, I knew that as soon as Clarice found out that I was earning money, she would probably develop a sudden need for extra cash. My fear was that if I brought my money home, I would one day find my money jar empty, which is why I kept it on top of the fridge on Andy El's porch, where I knew it was safe.

I sighed and looked around the trailer. It looked like there had been an explosion in a majorette costume factory.

Even though the second bedroom of the trailer was supposed to be the sewing room, somehow the whole living room had been taken over with patterns, fabric, pinned-together half-made costumes, and finished ones hanging all over on every spare spot. Sequins were everywhere.

Years before, I had been moved out of my bedroom to create the sewing room when Clarice got rid of my crib, which I had slept in until I was three.

My small dresser was shoved into the corner in the sewing room, but from that time on I slept on the couch, and I learned early to scrunch up my blanket and pillow in the morning and stuff them into the closet in the sewing room.

But since this was a whole new batch of costumes she had to design and sew from scratch, the entire trailer had been taken over. That meant it was a chaotic mess. Clarice didn't seem to notice, though. She was oblivious to the chaos our trailer was always in.

There were at least twenty of the costumes to do, all different sizes, and the one overriding thing Clarice knew was that she couldn't screw up even one of them. Mrs. Bateman would be furious, and Clarice knew enough not to risk that happening. So I knew that Clarice would be trying to limit her drinking and would be working steadily on them, certainly at the beginning of each week, until they were all completed.

Clarice finished off a side seam on the costume she was sewing on the machine, clipped the hanging threads with her scissors, and said, "Dig around in the fridge, you should be able to find something. Or there's a box of chicken noodle soup in the cupboard, I think."

"Thanks, Clarice. I'll get something later, I guess. See ya later." I grabbed an old school notebook from the shelf in the sewing room, and I headed back out the door.

"See ya, kid!" I heard her yell after me. "Stay outta trouble!"

Sighing, I sat outside on the grass on the patch of scrubby lawn beside our trailer and looked around the park.

There was no set pattern to the trailer park, as it had just emerged slowly over time. Andy El's trailer came first, of course, when she and her husband bought it secondhand and moved it onto the property.

Next, a man her husband had worked with at a road paving company had asked if he could put a trailer on the land next to it, and he'd arranged to pay some rent for the space. Then Mr. and Mrs. Williams heard about it and asked if they could move a trailer onto the land too.

After a few years, there were fifteen trailers in all on the land, in an informal trailer park. Everybody had about twenty feet of land around their trailer, so they could have a little garden or patio or whatever. When the first man moved on, he left the trailer behind and told Andy El she could just have it. So Andy El went in and cleaned it up and rented it out. Now, she had three trailers that she rented out, including ours. Everyone was really good about paying rent in cash to Andy El. Except maybe Clarice. I knew that she had got behind on our rent at least a few times through the years.

I still held a faint memory about that from years before. It was when Clarice got fired from her job at the coffee shop where she had been waitressing, and as a result she got way behind in rent. Andy El was going to let that slide, to give her a break — until Raymond found out about it. That's when Raymond came marching over one afternoon to Clarice's trailer, knocked firmly on the door, and told Clarice that he wanted to have a word with her.

Then he knelt down to where I was playing quietly in the living room and said, "Say there, Truly, Andy El's got some fresh fry bread over at her place, and she said that she wanted you to go on over and get some. How 'bout you head on over there now?"

I promptly scrambled to my feet and headed out the door, without even asking Clarice. It never occurred to me that I should ask her if it was okay.

As I eagerly headed off, thinking of that warm fry bread, I heard Raymond begin to lecture Clarice on her responsibilities. It was the only time I ever heard Raymond raise his voice. Startled, I stopped and listened. Clarice tried to object, but Raymond shushed her and continued angrily on.

"You have a child to think of, Clarice. You need to start putting her first. And that does *not* mean that you can take advantage of Andy El's good nature. You already owe her three months' rent, so just what do you plan to do about that?"

Of course, Clarice started to wail, but Raymond just said, "Your tears won't work on me, Clarice. You should know that by now. Now, you pull yourself together and you face your responsibilities. That means going out and getting another job, paying back Andy El, paying all your bills, and providing properly for Truly."

That seemed to have an effect on Clarice, because she went out the next day and got her job at the local tavern. It took some time, but she got all caught up on her rent, and even remembered to buy a few groceries for me. For a few months anyway, and then it all went back to me scrambling for what I could find to eat in the fridge and fending for myself. But she never got behind on the rent again, at least not for very long.

She would still let other bills slide, though, like the phone bill. I learned not to rely on having a working phone in the place, as it was a luxury that came and went, depending on whether she could afford to get it reconnected when it got cut off. Which was okay, because if I needed to use a phone, I knew Andy El had one in her trailer. That never bothered me very much. I never had anybody to call anyway.

It was funny, I mused, how Raymond was Andy El's nephew and not her son, but he was always looking out for her, and somehow seemed to be looking out for me too, in his own quiet way.

I opened my notebook, took up my stubby pencil, and turned to an empty page near the back. I started a heading called "List of Clues." Under this I wrote all of the clues that I had come up with so far:

— Has Elvis-style sideburns and wears his hair like Elvis.
— Wears aviator sunglasses, just like Elvis.
— Has blue eyes.
— Has a ton of Elvis outfits.
— Loves peanut butter.
— Has a guitar.
— Is a musician, and was famous once.
— Says, "Thank you. Thank you very much," just like Elvis.
— Name is Aaron. (Elvis's middle name.)
— Last name: Kingsley. Like Presley. And like King. As in the King!

So there it was, in black and white. Ten very solid clues that pointed to Aaron Kingsley's true identity. He really was Elvis Presley. And he was alive and well and living at the Eagle Shores Trailer Park.

I would keep gathering clues to tell my dad, so he would want to come and see for himself that Elvis was alive and living right here.

But really, I mused, the big question was: why was Elvis Presley hiding out at the Eagle Shores Trailer Park here on Vancouver Island?

CHAPTER 7

The next day was even busier at the lemonade stand. Word had got out about Andy El's homemade jam being for sale, and I sold all of the jars on the table. I refilled the lemonade jug three times, and even sold four more of Mrs. Williams's books.

Between customers, I read the Miss Marple book, trying to take notice of how she used her skills of observation to solve the murder. By about three o'clock, I was pretty hot and worn out, and I figured that everyone who wanted lemonade had come by the stand today already, so I packed up the last of the books and cleaned up the stand. I washed the dishes and left them to dry in Andy El's drying rack beside her sink.

I headed down to Clarice's trailer and found her getting ready for work at the tavern. She was humming and happy, finishing her pre-work drink. The sewing must have gone well; I could see a stack of finished costumes on the table. The remaining ones were all pinned together, waiting on the couch to be sewn. That was a relief for me. Because if her sewing had gone badly, somehow Clarice would figure that I was to blame, even though I had stayed away from the trailer all day.

"You can find something in the fridge to eat when you get hungry," she said. "I'll be late tonight. I got a date after work!"

That meant either another meal of hot dogs or a boiled egg, which was the extent of my cooking skills. That was okay with me. I could go over to Andy El's later, as I knew that she had made some clam chowder earlier. And I knew there was always a place for me at her table, as she liked to say. The chowder was made with fresh clams that Esther and her girls had dug up on the beach earlier this morning. I had heard them all in her yard, laughing and chatting as they scrubbed the clams and shucked them under the tap by Andy El's outdoor worktable, which was an old Formica-topped kitchen table.

I didn't say anything to Clarice about the chowder, though. I sat on the edge of the couch quietly and watched as Clarice breezed through the trailer, finding her shoes, then her keys, and then, draining her clinking glass with a final gulp, she was finally ready.

"How do I look, kiddo?" she asked, as she peered in the mirror, checking her hair one last time.

"You look real pretty, Clarice," I said. She gave me a distracted smile, and then, with an "Oh shoot — my lipstick!" she rushed back to her jumbled bedroom for a frantic search.

It was weird to me that I didn't look much like Clarice. I never asked her about my dad, but I figured I must look like him. I knew that I was Clarice's daughter, though, because she wouldn't have put up with me if I was someone else's kid. That much I knew.

"Okay, stay outta trouble, Truly," she yelled as she headed out the door and off to work.

I was relieved that I could go over to Andy El's for that clam chowder. I knew there wasn't much in the fridge to eat, and anyway, it was best if I stayed clear of all of the sewing.

I was just heading over to Andy El's when I saw Elvis's gold Sun Bug pull up and park next to his trailer. Elvis got out, reached into the back seat, pulled out a couple of grocery bags from the Food Mart, then headed inside his trailer. I decided that I would take my time getting over to Andy El's and that I could start to hone my Miss Marple skills on the way.

So I sat on the grass by our trailer to kill some time and got busy making a daisy chain with some dandelions that grew in our unruly patch of lawn. I figured that would give

Elvis some time to put his groceries away, and then I would wander slowly over, making my way casually past his trailer. That way, I could be on the lookout for more clues.

After a few minutes, I thought that I could hear music coming from his trailer. I stretched casually, got up, tossed the daisy chain on the grass, and idly sauntered over behind his trailer. I pretended to be interested in Mrs. Williams's roses. All the while I was checking for more Elvis clues. The roses really did smell beautiful, sweet and musky in their well-cared-for garden bed.

The little living room window of his trailer was open, so I leaned in a bit to see if I could hear anything.

Singing. I could hear singing. Elvis was singing! And he was playing his guitar. I strained to hear what the song was. He was singing "Love Me Tender." I was impressed with how good he was. And boy, did he ever sound like himself. He sounded just like he did on the record.

What more proof did I need? My suspicions were right. He really was Elvis! And here he was, living under a secret identity in our trailer park. And after hearing his singing, I had another really big clue to add to my notebook.

Elated, I headed over to Andy El's for dinner. Raymond was there, and it was so hot that we all sat outside on the grass and each had big a bowl of her homemade clam chowder. Raymond had us laughing all through dinner. He had a gentle way of teasing that wasn't at all mean. Raymond's teasing was kind and showed that he really knew us well. We sat out in the dusk, laughing at the stories he told about working in a logging camp when he first left school. He made it sound like a lot of fun, but I knew that logging was hard and dangerous work.

When there was a lull in the conversation, I timidly asked him, "Why didn't you stick with it? It sounds like you had a lot of fun."

Raymond sighed and said slowly, as though carefully choosing his words, "Well, I was pretty young, just out of high school. At first it was a real adventure, being off on my own like that. It's real hard work. And dangerous. And not everyone there was happy having a Native guy in the camp. Even though I worked hard, there was a lot of prejudice, and that made it hard to be there so far away from home. At least I earned enough money to go to college over in Vancouver. So, I headed off to the big city, and school, and then discovered that I was happier being home here at Eagle Shores, where my family is."

We sat for a few moments, each of us reflecting on his words, and then Andy El announced that we were going to make more strawberry jam. Raymond stood up and said with a quick wink at me, "Well, that's my cue to head on home!"

Andy El wrapped up some pieces of fry bread for Raymond to take home and insisted he take some clam chowder too.

"You brought me all that salmon last week," she said. "You make sure you got some chowder for tomorrow."

"What, you're not inviting me back for dinner again tomorrow night?" he teased, and then he gave her a hug and a kiss. "Bye, Mama, and thanks," he said, and, turning to me, he ruffled my hair and said, "See ya, Truly. Make sure you get her secret recipe for making jam!" and with that he headed off, walking home through the Cut.

After he had gone, Andy El put me to work helping her with another batch of strawberry jam. She set up a big cooking pot on a camp stove in the back yard, and set the berries and sugar bubbling away. Then she got some apples, skinned them, and had me grate them up.

"Some people use stuff called pectin when they make jam, but you gotta buy that at the store," she explained. "My mama taught me how to make jam this way, with apples. They cook up and dissolve, and they make your jam just as thick as the stuff you buy. Apples got that pectin stuff in them, so they make jam real good and thick."

I carefully added the grated apple to the jam. While it simmered, Andy El broke up some bars of paraffin wax and put them into an old battered pot, which she put inside a bigger pot, which was partially filled with water.

"You got to be real careful with the wax, Truly," she explained. "You melt it like this inside another pot of water. Never put a pot of wax right on the burner." Then she kept her eye on both the melting wax and the cooking jam.

My next job was washing the dishes. First I washed all the dinner dishes, then I dried them and put them all away. I loved how tidy Andy El kept her trailer. Everything had its own place, and you always knew where a certain pot or dish was. It was not at all like Clarice's trailer, which was in a constant state of chaos. Even if Clarice ever did decide to put a dish away, I don't think she would know where to start in our little kitchen.

I put the leftover clam chowder in the fridge. There would be enough for lunch or dinner tomorrow night too.

Then I washed all of the canning jars and made sure they were rinsed out well. I shuttled them outside to Andy El's outdoor worktable. I set them up carefully, so they were all ready to be filled. When Andy El decided the jam was all cooked, she carefully ladled it into each jar. Once they were all filled, she wiped the edge of each jar with a clean cloth.

Then she carefully took the melted wax off of the burner and put the pot down on a mat on the table. She showed me how to carefully lay a piece of string across the opening of each jar and then snip it so that there was about two inches dangling over each side. And then once I was done laying string across the top of the jam in each one, I stepped back and watched as she carefully poured the melted wax into the mouth of each jar to seal it.

"That string'll make it easier for folks to pull the wax out when they want to open the jam," she explained. "The wax keeps the jam sealed off from the air so it won't go bad."

"There now," she said. "We'll just wait till they all cool, and then we'll put lids on them."

I counted the jars of jam. We had made fourteen more jars of jam. The wax was already starting to harden, and it formed a seal on the jam about a quarter of an inch thick.

I loved working with Andy El. I learned so much from her that I never did with Clarice. Andy El actually cooked things from scratch. She was always making fry bread, soups and chowders, and canning vegetables from her garden. Way more than just boiling eggs or hot dogs, or heating up stuff from a can like Clarice did.

As we waited for the jars to cool, I figured I'd better make some more ice cubes for tomorrow's lemonade. I opened the fridge out on the porch and pulled out the metal ice cube tray. I took it to the sink and refilled the empty squares where ice was missing, so we would have plenty for lemonade.

With a satisfied sigh, Andy El sat down on the porch couch

to knit. She was working on a new winter vest for Esther's son, Edgar Jr., using thick wool and large needles. Andy El was a beautiful knitter, and she often sold sweaters and vests that she'd knitted. There was always someone stopping by her trailer getting measured up by Andy El, and they would look at her wool colors and designs so they could choose how their sweater or hat would look. Her wools were thick like rope and came in natural colors of cream, dark brown, or gray.

This one was a cream color. On the back, Andy El had added the image of a huge thunderbird in dark brown wool, and there would be two leaping salmon on the front. She said that was to bring him good luck when he was out fishing.

I loved to watch her knit and listen to the clicking of the needles as they dove in and out of the wool. The patterns emerged quickly as we sat together.

"'Bout time I started teaching you to knit," she commented, and I grinned at her. Andy El had more plans for me already. It did look satisfying to do. "This coming winter, I think we'll get you started knitting. You're about the age I started all my girls knitting."

"I think that would be pretty cool, Andy El," I said. I continued to watch her flying fingers for a while, and then pulled out my notebook and added to my Elvis clue list:

— Plays guitar.

— Sings Elvis songs.

— Sings just like Elvis.

The clues were piling up, and so was the proof that Aaron Kingsley really was Elvis Presley. But why was he here at Eagle Shores? I tucked the notebook away where I knew it would be safe, under the plaid couch on the porch. Then I sat as Andy El continued to knit and read my Miss Marple book. I figured that I needed all the tips I could get to be a good detective. Besides, it was a real good book.

CHAPTER 8

I must have fallen asleep on the couch, because when I woke up it was morning. I was covered up with a blanket, and a pillow had been slipped under my head.

It was another beautiful, sunny day, and I was filled with happiness. I should have known that wouldn't last. For me, happiness was always a fleeting thing. Something would always go horribly wrong to wreck any good thing that came along for me.

On the kitchenette stove was a pot of oatmeal that Andy El had left warming for me. I served myself a big bowl, sprinkled some brown sugar on top, and poured milk over it. I sat and had my breakfast, then washed my dishes carefully and set them in the rack to dry.

Then I got the first jug of lemonade made up and got out the ice cube tray. I held it over the sink, and, pulling the creaking metal lever, I cracked the ice cubes apart. I dumped them into the jug and gave it a good stir. Then I refilled the cube tray and carefully walked across the kitchen and out onto the porch to put the filled tray back in the freezer. We'd need to keep up on the ice cube supply, I figured.

Andy El was already out in her vegetable garden, weeding and watering before it got too hot.

"Morning, sleepy-head!" she called, waving a handful of green beans at me. I saw that she had set the tablecloth out on the lemonade stand so it was all ready for me. I waved to her, grinning.

I took the jug and glasses out and then set out the jars of jam and the stack of books. I put out my signs and pulled up my rickety lawn chair to sit on and wait for customers. It had all the signals of being a beautiful day.

Mrs. Williams was my first customer of the day, as she always walked out early to get her mail.

"My, that sure hits the spot," she said as she finished the glass. She looked at the table for a moment, and then added, "I may just have some more books for you, if you wish. They do seem to be going fast, don't they?"

"Well, sure, that would be great. Thanks, Mrs. Williams," I said. What the heck, I thought, it would help me earn more money in the end. And people did seem to be buying them.

She headed off to her trailer and then came back a few minutes later with another six books. I saw that two more were Miss Marple. With any luck I could read them quickly, before they sold.

Later that morning I looked up from my book to see Elvis walking over to my stand from his trailer. He bought a glass of lemonade, then thumbed through the stack of books. He bought one of them. I held my breath as he chose, sighing in relief as he put aside the Miss Marple.

And then he looked straight at me with those blue eyes and asked me something that made my blood run cold.

"I understand that your mama takes in sewing, is that right, Truly?" he asked. "I have a repair job I need done on one of my outfits, and I need someone who is good with sequins. I hear tell that your mama is real good at that, is that right?"

My heart plunged. Up until now, I had considered Elvis and his secret life at Eagle Shores to be my big secret too. No one else at the trailer park could see that it was really him, and even though I knew the truth, his secret was safe with me.

And I knew that as soon as Clarice met him, that would all change. I knew Clarice. Even though she had a new guy in the picture, I knew that she was always on the lookout for a better option. With a sinking heart, I knew that she would consider Elvis Presley a way, way better option than anybody she'd ever dated up till now.

So far their paths hadn't crossed, mainly because Elvis kept normal hours and stayed in his trailer most days.

Clarice worked late at night, slept in, and of course had been stuck in our trailer, busily sewing up a storm with those majorette costumes. But as soon as they were all finished, I knew that she would be out on the little patch of lawn by our trailer on a blanket in her bathing suit sunning herself every afternoon till she got ready for work, with her transistor radio blaring.

And now, if Elvis needed her to do a sewing job, she would see exactly who he was, and she would let the whole world know. His secret would be out, and he'd have to leave Eagle Shores and move on.

I knew that Clarice would take one look at him and would try flirting and flaunting around him. Even worse, he might just fall for her, too. Until he realized just what she was like. And then he would start to think badly of me, too.

My heart sunk so low, I swear it was digging itself a pit right into the ground by my feet.

But I couldn't lie to Elvis. I had to tell him the truth, no matter the consequences. He was Elvis Presley, after all. The King. I couldn't lie to Elvis. Besides, I knew that Andy El would never put up with lying. I knew she expected better than that from me, and I couldn't let her down. Of course, when it came to the trip to Vancouver to meet my dad, I told myself that I wasn't lying to Andy El. I just wasn't telling her about it, until I was safely on the ferry and she read my note.

But right now, between the King and Andy El, I had no choice. I had to tell Elvis the truth.

Resigned, I said, "Yes, my mom does sewing. And she's real good with sequins. Right now, though, she's sewing a whole bunch of majorette costumes, but I think in a few days they'll be nearly all done."

He smiled that famous Elvis smile and said, "Well, that sounds real good to me. That sounds like it'll work out about just right for what I need, in fact."

I didn't even think that Clarice had come home last night, since I hadn't seen her car all morning. I had slept at Andy El's, so I couldn't be sure.

I tried to sound cheerful when I said to him, "I don't think my mom is home right now. I can check with her about when would be a good time for you to talk to her about a sewing job. I think it'll be at least a few days, though."

He nodded and said, "That's fine, there's no real rush. I won't need that outfit for a while." He turned to walk away, and then he looked back at me with another big Elvis Presley smile and said, "Thank you. Thank you very much," and headed back to his trailer.

I sighed. I was pretty well out of lemonade at that point,

so I figured I'd better go see if Clarice was home and, if so, what state she was in. I poured the last of the lemonade into a glass and gulped it down.

I headed over with the empty jug and glasses and saw that Clarice's car was now parked beside the trailer, so I knew that unless she had gone off with her new boyfriend in his car, she was home. I carefully opened the door to our trailer and stepped inside.

Clarice was slouched on the couch, smoking a cigarette and drinking a coffee. She looked pretty rough. Last night's makeup was smudged all around her eyes, making them look dark and sore. Obviously, Clarice's temporary attempt at staying sober so that she could be clear-headed while she sewed the costumes had gone off the rails, certainly as of last night.

"Hi," I said casually, still trying to get a read on Clarice's mood. I stayed near the door, in case I needed to clear out fast. But she wasn't too mad at me this morning.

"Hey, Truly," she said in a raspy voice, taking a deep drag on her cigarette. "How's tricks?"

"Good," I said cautiously. I was still getting a feel for things.

"So, word is that you're runnin' a lemonade stand this summer. That true?" she asked, exhaling a cloud of smoke.

"Well, yeah," I said. "Really, it's more for Andy El." I figured that wasn't really too big a lie, as I had started out doing the stand to make Andy El happy. Besides, lying to Clarice wasn't really lying. It was more about my survival. I didn't want her to know that I was earning money.

She shrugged, obviously not too interested, which was a relief. "So long as you stay outta trouble, Truly, do whatever." she said and stretched, yawning. So far, her mood wasn't too bad.

I knew that I had to ask about sewing for Elvis. I hated to do this, because who knew what this would unleash in Clarice, but I had promised Elvis. I took a deep breath, braced myself, and started with: "So, how are the costumes coming?"

"Good, actually. I think I should be all done in a few more days," she said. "Then I can get rid of them and drop them off to the old battle-axe."

So far, so good, I thought, figuring it was as safe a time as any. At least right now, Clarice was actually listening to me, so this was probably the best time to bring it up.

"So, there's a new tenant here, renting a trailer from Andy El," I began, trying to sound as casual as I could. "He asked me to check if you could do some sewing for him. He says he has some repairs he needs to have done to some sequinned suit or something."

Clarice stretched, and then made a face and said, "A

guy with a sequinned suit? What is he, a country singer or something? Geez, that's all we need around here."

"I guess so, something like that," I said. Again, not a real lie.

"Well, lemme get these damned costumes finished off and outta my hair. Then I can see him one afternoon sometime, before I have to go to work," she said. She yawned again, and added, "Then I can see just what it's gonna take, to fix his damned cowboy suit!"

"Sure, I'll let him know if I see him around. He said there's no rush," I said, and I slipped out of the trailer, flooded with relief. I knew it was just a temporary reprieve. I knew in my heart it was only a matter of time till Clarice met Elvis, set her sights on him, and ruined everything.

CHAPTER 9

I headed back to Andy El's. I washed the glasses, and then made more lemonade, filling the jug with ice cubes and then refilling the ice cube tray. I took the jug out to the stand, and then ran back for the glasses.

I set them out and waited for my customers, trying to tell myself that it wasn't the end of the world. But I couldn't help feeling real blue.

That afternoon, Esther and her daughters, Agnes and Linda, came over with three more really big salmon for Andy El. They were really proud that their older brother Edgar had caught the salmon and was doing well with his first season working as a fisherman.

The twins came over to the stand shyly and asked how much the lemonade was. I told them they could have a glass each on the house, as they were Andy El's granddaughters, and she'd done so much to get me started in business.

"But just this once," I cautioned. "I gotta make money from this stand," I explained.

They sat on the grass, sipping their lemonade. Agnes got up and looked through the stack of books.

"Hey," she said, "these are all Agatha Christie books. I love these books!"

"You know about Agatha Christie books?" I was surprised. I had never heard of them before Mrs. Williams had brought them to my table.

"Well, sure, everybody knows these books," she said. She saw my face and then quickly added, "Well, I just assumed everybody has, just 'cause I have. Silly of me, I guess, huh?"

Linda grinned and said, "Agnes always has her nose in a book!" She laughed and shoved Agnes in a friendly, teasing way.

Agnes retorted with, "Oh yeah? Well, not everybody is happy chasing around after a soccer ball, either!"

Watching them tease each other that way that made me feel like a real outsider. I wondered, not for the first time, what it must be like to have a sister or a brother. *I bet they never get lonely*, I thought.

It was funny: as close as I was to Andy El, and I knew Esther and Raymond pretty well, I didn't really know Agnes and Linda very well at all.

They attended the tribal school right on the reserve, and I went by bus to the local school in town. All of a sudden, I felt shy around them. Crazy, even though I'd known them for most of my life. But I had never really spent a lot of time with them. I just saw them casually when they came over to visit Andy El, and when they did, I usually made myself scarce. After all, they really were Andy El's granddaughters, and I was just an outsider.

We sat quietly for a few moments, until Agnes asked, "So, are you going to the parade next Saturday?" I had forgotten that the Newman Bay Days parade and town festival would be happening so soon.

"I guess so," I said. "I hadn't really given it much thought. I probably have to go and help Mrs. Bateman hand out batons and stuff to all of the majorettes. She lets them use really special ones with streamers just for the parade and competitions."

"We're going!" Linda said excitedly. "Uncle Raymond is taking us to town for the parade, and we might get to go over to the fair after for a while!"

"Maybe we could all go together," said Agnes.

"Sure, that would be great," I said. But I didn't really mean it. I knew there would be no money from Clarice for me to go to the fair, and I sure wasn't going to part with any of my hard-earned lemonade stand money for a ride or cotton candy, no matter how fun it sounded. I had to save all of my money to go Vancouver and meet my dad and tell him that Elvis was living at the trailer park.

Just then, Andy El came out of her trailer with a salmon wrapped up in newspaper. She handed it to me, saying, "I want you to take this over to Mrs. Wyman at the farm. I owe her for all those extra berries she gave to me."

She said to Agnes and Linda, "Why don't you girls go too? You can see them puppies. And you can see the one that Truly's gonna buy."

The twins got all excited when they heard about the puppies, so then I had to explain about my plan to save money from my lemonade stand for the puppy. I wasn't too comfortable with Andy El spilling the beans like that, especially as it wasn't really true.

"Don't you worry, I can watch the stand," said Andy El. "Me and Esther can sit out here and take a break from cleanin' fish!"

We got up, the twins still all excited to see the puppies, and we headed down the road to the Wymans' farm.

When we got there, I knocked on the farmhouse back door, and then waited. After a few moments, Mrs. Wyman opened it. When she saw the big salmon Andy El had sent us with, she got a huge smile on her face.

"Well, this is great!" she said. "I wasn't expecting another one so soon!" Then she looked past me at the twins, who hung back shyly on the driveway, and said in a really kind voice, "Hello there, you're Esther's girls, aren't you?"

They nodded politely, keeping their eyes lowered.

"Truly, why don't you take the girls into the barn to see the puppies?" she suggested. "I'll be right out as soon as I put this in the fridge."

The door closed behind her, and the three of us headed into the barn, me leading the way. I felt important as I explained to them how to slowly approach Lady and let her sniff their hands.

Then I knelt down, stroked the little brown puppy on the head, and then picked him up gently.

"Oh," breathed Agnes. "They're so cute!"

The puppy had already grown since I had seen him last. I snuggled him close. If only I really could be saving to buy him, like I was telling everyone. It would be so nice to have a dog. But I knew it could never happen.

"You're so lucky, Truly," said Linda. I felt a pang of guilt. But, I told myself, I was lucky in another way. When I found my dad and told him all about Elvis, he would want to come back to us and stay at Eagle Shores. And maybe we could really get a dog.

The twins sat and gently petted all of the scrambling puppies, and laughed delightedly at their puppy antics.

After a few moments, Mrs. Wyman came into the barn, and the twins stood up quietly and moved back from the puppies. I could tell that they were nervous being in the barn, seeing as the Wymans were white folks and all. I saw that Agnes and Linda were braced and waiting to see how they would be treated before they could relax. They just slipped into it, like putting on a protective jacket.

I reluctantly put my pup down, after whispering quietly to him, "Sorry, puppy, you can't really go home with me! But I know the Wymans will find you a good home." I stood up too, and we all thanked Mrs. Wyman politely for letting us see the puppies.

She smiled at us kindly and said, "Well, you girls thank Andy El for that lovely salmon!" Then she added, "How's the lemonade stand going, Truly?"

"Things are going great! I've saved five dollars and forty cents so far!" I said proudly.

She nodded at me and seemed pleased. "Well, that's just great, Truly. I really mean that."

Then she picked up another big basket of berries from the table, saying, "You girls take these to Andy El, will you please? That salmon is much larger than I expected, and I feel I owe her more berries in exchange."

Then she picked up a small pint basket and handed it to Agnes, smiling kindly.

"And here's one you girls can snack on on the way back to Eagle Shores. That way, I know Andy El's strawberries will get to her safely!"

We all thanked her and headed back to the trailer park, eating the sweet berries as we went.

"She sure is nice for a white lady," said Linda. "And you sure are lucky to be getting a dog." I said hesitantly, "Look, I want to ask you a favor. Please don't tell anyone about my dog plan." They stopped and looked at me in surprise.

"How come?" asked Agnes. "If it was me, I'd be yelling it out all over the place!"

"Well, I haven't told Clarice about it yet," I said. "I haven't figured out the best way to tell her. But I know it'll be okay. I'm going to earn the money for his food and everything else. She won't have to worry about it costing extra money." I looked down at the ground, sort of ashamed. "It's just — well, you know how Clarice can get." They both nodded, understanding, and I felt much better. But as nice as they both were, I knew that I couldn't tell them that I wasn't really going to buy the puppy or that I was secretly saving my lemonade stand money for my trip to Vancouver to find my dad. That had to stay a secret from everyone, even Andy El.

"Come on," said Linda, "we better get these berries to Andy El before we eat all of hers too!"

We raced each other back to Eagle Shores, laughing, trying not to spill the berries down the sun-filled road.

We arrived back on the reserve and got to the lemonade

stand at the same time as a man pulled up in a big red car with the radio blaring some awful disco song. He swept right by us, and pulled up at Clarice's trailer. We watched as Clarice came out and climbed in beside him.

The car turned around and headed up the driveway towards us again. Clarice sat snuggled up tight to the driver, who had his arm draped around her shoulders. *So this must be her new conquest*, I thought to myself. And my heart dropped to the earth again.

CHAPTER 10

"Hey, a lemonade stand!" the guy said, glancing casually out the window at us. "Want some, babe?"

"No thanks, I'll pass," said Clarice brightly. She didn't look at me. She didn't look at any of us. She just squinted out at the stand of trees across the road as though we weren't even there.

"Good call," he said, staring at Andy El and Esther. "They probably can't even read the can to make it right anyway!"

We could hear Clarice's laughter as they drove away. My eyes dropped to the ground, and I couldn't look at anyone. The flashy car drove away, fishtailing and spraying gravel as it turned onto the road. Some of the gravel even splattered onto the lemonade stand.

We were all silent. I could feel Esther's anger building.

"It's not right, Andy El, to be treated like that on our own land!" Esther muttered quietly. "Bad enough to get treated like that in town."

"You hush now!" said Andy El. She shot a strong look

at her. Then Andy El turned to us girls and said cheerfully, as though nothing had happened, "So, now, what's with all these berries? And tell me 'bout them puppies!" And Agnes and Linda, both talking at once, told her and Esther how Mrs. Wyman had said the salmon was so big that it wasn't a fair trade, and so she sent another big basket of strawberries home with us to make it a more even trade.

Then, with Andy El laughing and asking questions, Agnes and Linda described the puppies and how cute they were. Me and Esther, though, we just sat, both of us quiet. Esther, I could tell, was still really mad about how rude Clarice and her boyfriend had been, whereas I was just — kind of numb.

After a time, Andy El suggested that we close up shop early and pack up the stand. They all helped me get the stand squared away for the day. I was relieved, as I knew it was to distract everyone from what had just happened with Clarice and her boyfriend.

We headed back to Andy El's, and Esther and the girls headed for home. I heard Esther whisper to Andy El, "I still don't like this, Mama, not at all! It's not right!"

Andy El patted her hand and said, "It'll all be okay, you'll see. Always is, somehow." Esther sighed and kissed Andy El's wrinkled cheek.

"You always see the best in everyone, Mama," she said. "I

love you for that." Then she smiled and added, "Guess I gotta give that a try sometime!" and they both laughed.

After they left, Andy El said, "Looks like we got some work to do making more jam, Truly! I got some more jars in a box, out in my shed somewheres. You go get 'em and start washing, while I start the jam cooking. Just hope I got enough sugar for it!"

I headed off to her jumbled shed and rummaged around for the box of jars. I found the box on top of an old dresser, so I picked it up and headed back to Andy El's trailer.

My heart felt full of stones, it was so heavy. It was only then that I realized that Clarice hadn't bothered to introduce me to her boyfriend. That meant they were still in the honeymoon phase, and Clarice hadn't told him about me yet.

CHAPTER 11

I slept at Andy El's again and woke up to birds singing cheerfully outside and Andy El humming in the kitchen. I stretched, yawned, then forced myself to get up.

I headed inside and was greeted with, "Good morning, you sleepy thing. Good thing you got up. I thought that I was gonna have to go shake you!"

She put a plate of warm fry bread and a scrambled egg in front of me, and proudly said, "I can give you another six jars of jam to sell outta the batch we made last night."

I looked at her gratefully. I ate quickly, then got washed. Then I got to work making lemonade, adding ice, and making sure I refilled the ice cube tray.

Then I went out into the sunshine and set up the table. I glanced at Clarice's trailer and was relieved to see that her boyfriend's car wasn't in sight, and her car was parked there. At least if she was home, it meant that she was alone.

I would give her some time before I headed over, though. I knew if she was home, she would be sleeping late. And I knew not to wake her up.

Mrs. Williams was my first customer, and then Mr. Wyman came by again for a glass. "I've been thinking about this lemonade all morning, working out in the fields," he said. "Sure does hit the spot!"

It was pretty busy all morning, and by lunchtime I had sold out two jugs. I barely had any time to read my Miss Marple, but I got the book finished in the early afternoon. I closed the cover and put it back on the stack of books for sale, thinking about what I had read. How the heck had that old lady known all that stuff about people, enough to know who the murderer was? I had tried as I read through the book to guess who the bad guy was, but I didn't even come close.

I sighed. Maybe being a detective wasn't as easy as I'd thought it would be. *I need to keep working at this, to become a good detective*, I thought to myself. *After all, Miss Marple was an old lady, so maybe it takes all those years to hone your skills.*

That was when Elvis came up for a glass of lemonade, and I remembered about his sewing request.

As he drank the lemonade, I said hesitantly, "So, I asked my mom yesterday about your sewing job. She should be all finished the majorette costumes by next week, and she could fit yours in sometime after that, if that's okay with you."

And then I had a flash of inspiration.

"You know," I said, "Clarice is really busy with sewing all those majorette costumes. So, if you need your repair done sooner, there's another place in town that does sewing repairs and hemming and stuff like that. At the dry cleaner's in town," I suggested hopefully. "It's called Mason's One Day Martinizing, and I hear they pride themselves on reliability and fine-quality workmanship."

I didn't know that for sure; I was simply quoting the faded fly-speckled sign in the window of their dry cleaner's shop. I did know that they could be counted on to undertake a sewing job on any day of the week, not just Monday to Wednesday, or Thursday noon at the very latest. They could be counted on to sew with accuracy right up till Saturday afternoon.

Mr. and Mrs. Mason owned the store. They were members of the Newman Bay Rotary Club, regularly went to church, and, I had heard it said, only drank socially, so their late in the week sewing and dry cleaning jobs had never fallen victim to any spontaneous overindulging, as did so many of Clarice's. I didn't know what social drinking was, but I was pretty sure it wasn't anything like the way Clarice drank.

Elvis just smiled at me and said, "That's real kind of you to think of that for me, but there's no rush for it, Truly. I hear your mama's real good at sewing, and I'm sure she could use the work, so I don't mind waiting till she has time to do it."

I sighed, resigned. "Okay," I said, "I'll check with her again and let you know when she's got them all done."

"That'll be just fine, Truly, thank you," he said, and headed back to his trailer. I stared glumly after him. I had tried my best to save him from Clarice, but it wasn't much consolation. I knew that it didn't really matter that she wasn't an Elvis fan. Clarice was a fan of a new possible conquest, and Elvis was right here at the trailer park.

CHAPTER 12

Next day, I had set up my stand by nine o'clock, and I was just putting out the books and six more jars of Andy El's jam when Mrs. Marshall came up with a cookie tin and a pile of paper napkins in her hands.

"Good morning, Truly," she said. "I'll have my usual," and she giggled at her own joke. I poured her a glass of lemonade and handed it to her.

She put the cookie tin on the table, opened the clasp on her little red leather change purse, and fished out a dime.

Then she said, "You know, Truly, I was up early baking this morning, and I got a bit carried away. So I had an idea. I made all these blueberry muffins, way more than I could ever eat myself, and I thought that you could put them out for sale, so folks could have a muffin with their lemonade." She opened the tin and showed me one dozen freshly baked muffins.

And then she leaned down and whispered, "I'll donate

these to the cause. You can earn more money for your puppy fund!"

"Oh, gee." I didn't know what to say. "Thanks, that's really nice of you!" I said.

She looked at my now overflowing table, and added, "You know, I have an old card table that you can have, too."

She headed back to her trailer and came back a moment later with a collapsible card table with black metal legs and a dark green top. She showed me how to set it up and said, "There, that'll give you lots of room to spread things out."

Then she patted my arm, and said, "I think it's just wonderful that you're working so hard, Truly, and saving for a puppy. We're all rooting for you!" Then she added briskly, "Well now, I'd better get on with my day, or I'll get nothing done!" and she headed back to her trailer.

I sat, amazed, looking at those beautiful muffins. Her words echoed in my head: "We're all rooting for you!" I was overwhelmed at the thought that some of the other residents actually cared that I got my puppy.

Although, it worried me that now so many people thought that I was saving for a puppy. Still, it made me feel really warm inside to think that somehow I wasn't just some annoying little twerp who lurked around the trailer park. I spent so much of my time avoiding Clarice and trying to stay out of the way of all her boyfriends that I guess I had never really taken the time to look around and see that some of the residents might actually like me, and even care about me. Beyond Andy El, of course.

The muffins, the jam jars, and the whole lemonade stand dissolved before me into a blur of tears. Then I wiped my eyes, pulled out my spy notebook, and pulled out a page to make a new sign: *Fresh Baked Blueberry Muffins 10 cents.*

Then I rushed over to the trailer to tell Andy El the good news. She gave me a huge hug and said, "That's just so nice, Truly. You really are gonna get your puppy money all saved up by the end of the summer, just you wait and see!"

I couldn't help feeling a small pang of guilt. I was still letting Andy El think that I was saving for a puppy. I knew that she would never let me go to Vancouver on my own to find my dad, so I had to keep it a secret.

I headed back to the stand and sat expectantly, waiting for more customers. And that's when Elvis walked over.

"Mornin', Truly," he said. "Say, blueberry muffins! I better get some of those," he added as he scanned the table. He had a glass of lemonade and then bought two of the muffins. I wrapped them carefully in a napkin for him, and handed them to him.

As he drank his glass of lemonade, I braced myself and said, "Um, Mr. Kingsley? I'll check with Clarice today and see when she can do that sewing job for you."

"Well, that would be real great. Because it looks like I'm gonna need that outfit pretty soon, after all."

I was reluctant to remind Clarice about the sewing job, but I couldn't think of another way out. He had asked for my help. And you couldn't let someone like Elvis Presley down.

Then he leaned down and whispered, "Can you keep a secret? I'm gonna be in the Newman Bay Days parade. The Chamber of Commerce has hired me to perform! They got a float all ready for me, and I'll be up there singin' and playin' my guitar! It's gonna be a bit of a surprise to everybody, cause nobody knows that I'm here. But they sure will after that parade!" With that, he headed back to his trailer, whistling a familiar tune. As I listened, I realized the song was "That's All Right."

But it wasn't all right with me. Not at all. Now everyone would know that he was the real Elvis Presley, and his secret would be out. Now everything would change.

I sat glumly. What a morning! I had gone from being so elated such a short time ago to being back down in the dumps and dreading what was coming next. But that was the way things went for me. Something good happened, and instead of enjoying it and feeling all happy, I had learned that I should just be on the lookout for the next tough luck break. Because something would always come along to ruin the good for me, that much I knew.

After a while, I could hear the radio in our trailer blaring, so I knew Clarice was up. I went to Andy El's and asked her if she could watch my stand for a while, and then I went down to remind Clarice about Elvis's request.

I opened the trailer door and saw with relief that Clarice seemed to be in a fairly good mood, singing along with the radio and sorting out the costumes, which were all finished. She was folding them and packing them into boxes.

"Hey, Truly," she said absentmindedly.

"Hey, Clarice," I said. I stood watching her for a few minutes as she folded the top down on the last box.

"There!" she said, hands on her hips. "Those damned things are done! And that gets the old battle-axe off my back for a while, at least!"

She started clearing up the last of the sewing mess of bright blue and white sequins and bits of leftover royal blue satiny fabric. She shoved them all in a box, and I knew that she would repurpose it all somehow, turning the bits into some outfit for herself or adding what she called "some glitz" to something she already had.

As I stood there, I tried to think of something that she had ever sewed for me, but I couldn't remember anything. Maybe she had when I was a baby, and of course it would make sense that I didn't remember. These days all my clothes, such as they were, came from a thrift store or, sometimes, bags of hand-me-downs that she was given by friends of Mrs. Bateman. Or things that Andy El picked up here and there for me.

I cleared my throat. I had to do this, as much as I hated to. *For Elvis*, I reminded myself.

"So, that new tenant, Mr. Kingsley, he asked again about that sewing repair. I guess he needs it for the Newman Bay Days Parade. He's gonna be performing on a float."

I couldn't understand why Elvis Presley had come all this way to hide himself away in a little trailer park on Vancouver Island, and now, after such a short time, he was about to announce to the whole world that he was really alive and well. Maybe he was already tired of hiding away from the world and wanted his old life back. I really needed to get to Vancouver and find my dad to let him know that Elvis was here.

Clarice sighed, looked at her wrist watch, and said, "Oh, all right, tell him to come over anytime now. I might as well get it done before I go out again this afternoon. The sooner I get these damned costumes out of my hands, the better!" She smiled brightly. "Got another date tonight!"

I stood for a moment, and then said, "So, that was him in the car, the other day? Your new boyfriend?"

She lit a cigarette, waved the match out, and said, "Yep, this one's a real good looker, huh, kid?"

And that was it. No explanation about why she had let him be rude to Andy El and her family, or why she hadn't bothered to introduce us all to him.

I sighed and headed out to Elvis's trailer with a heavy heart to give him Clarice's message.

CHAPTER 13

As I got close, I could hear him playing the guitar and singing — he was rehearsing again! I crept closer and noticed that his door was open; just the screen door on the trailer was closed. I discovered that if I stood at an angle, I could watch him.

He was singing "All Shook Up," playing the guitar, and shaking his hips and dancing at the same time. No wonder they called him the King! He really was the King of Rock and Roll. It was just like one of his movies I had watched on our TV.

We used to have an old black and white TV at the trailer, but eventually the picture tube had burned out, and Clarice had said, "Well, so much for that old thing" and unplugged it and lugged it out for garbage pickup at the side of the road, where all the residents put out their trash cans once a week. Andy El didn't have a TV, so it was something that I had only faint memories of watching. But I do remember seeing an old Elvis movie, with everyone dancing on the beach. And, peeking into his trailer, I sure thought he looked just like the Elvis Presley from that movie.

When he finished the song, he put his guitar down, wiped his brow with a scarf he had around his neck, and took a drink of water from a glass on the table. I gave him a few minutes and then knocked and waited for him to come to the door.

"Well, hey there, Truly," he said when he saw it was me. I acted real casual, so that he would assume that I hadn't heard or seen him rehearsing. I had told him that I could keep a secret, and I wanted to prove that I could.

"Hi, Mr. Kingsley, I talked to Clarice — my mom — and she's done those costumes already, so she says you should head over anytime this afternoon to bring her the repair job," I said. "She's going out later, so she said even now is fine with her."

"Well, that's just great." He beamed at me. "I can just grab my jumpsuit now, and you can take me over and introduce me to her. Give me just a minute." He disappeared into the bedroom of the trailer and came back with his dry cleaning bag.

My heart sank. I could sure keep a secret, but Elvis didn't seem to care about being discreet at all. Here he was, about to march through the whole trailer park carrying a dry cleaning bag with a flashy jumpsuit.

I braced myself and led the way over to our trailer, so I could introduce him to Clarice. I was relieved to see that no one else was outside, so no one was there to see Elvis with that classic Elvis Presley outfit. Otherwise, it would have been a dead giveaway as to his identity.

I opened up our trailer door and called out, "Hey, Clarice, Mr. Kingsley is here with his mending job!"

Clarice came out of the sewing room, a cigarette in her hand.

"Well, come on in, Mr. Kingsley," she said. "You can call me Clarice!"

Elvis stepped inside and said, "Pleased to meet you. Please, call me Aaron. Truly tells me you're a good seamstress and can do a real good job with sequins."

Of course, Clarice took one real good look at Elvis and got all giggly and flirty. I just looked down at my feet, getting red-faced with shame. You would never believe for a minute that she claimed she couldn't stand Elvis Presley the way she was gushing all over him.

She stubbed out her cigarette in an ashtray that was already overflowing on the kitchen table and said, with a coy smile and a wink, "Well, Aaron, let's see what you got for me!"

He ignored that and just carefully peeled back the plastic bag and showed her where the sequins had started to pull away from the fabric in places, and where the seam on one of the wide lapels was coming apart.

"Can you repair this, do you think?" he said. "I'd like to wear this next Saturday."

"Oh, sure, I can do this easy!" said Clarice. "I can get it all done by the day after tomorrow, no problem! Why don't you stop by and see if it's ready?" she suggested. "Come by for a drink, about four o'clock, whatcha say?" she added hopefully. She gave him a really big smile and batted her eyes at him.

Elvis smiled, but it was just a very polite smile. "Well, that would be just great if you can get it done that soon for me. And that's a real nice offer, but I'm not sure I'll have time to stop by for a drink. I'm pretty busy rehearsing these days. Maybe you can just let Truly know when the sewing's all done, and how much the charge will be, and I can just stop by really quick and pick it up. Thank you. Thank you very much." Then he looked at me and smiled that kind, gentle smile he had. As though he was letting me know that he understood about how Clarice could be.

"Thank you too, Truly," he said, and added, "Well, I'd better get back to rehearsing."

And with that he turned and left the trailer.

Clarice was none too happy that Elvis had left that quickly. As a matter of fact, she seemed pretty annoyed at him for ignoring her not-too-subtle advances. I was relieved.

Not only was Clarice mad at Elvis, she hadn't even noticed who he was! I couldn't believe it, but I figured that it meant I must be a pretty good detective, way better than I had given myself credit for. Because apparently, I was still the only one around who could see that Aaron Kingsley really was the real Elvis Presley, alive and well and living at the Eagle Shores Trailer Park with all the rest of us regular people. The only mystery left to solve was why he was here, of all places?

I was so relieved when I made my way back to the lemonade stand to pack things up for the day, I realized that I was humming "All Shook Up." It really was a catchy tune.

CHAPTER 14

That night I actually slept at Clarice's trailer, since the sewing had all been cleared off the couch and I had a place to sleep again. I also didn't want to wear out my welcome at Andy El's trailer.

Clarice came in late that night, but she wasn't too loud, so I was able to roll over and get back to sleep as she muttered and stumbled through the trailer to her bedroom.

She was still asleep when I got up at about nine-thirty the next morning, so I got dressed and packed up my bedding as quietly as I could. I rolled up my blanket and pillow in a bundle and stuffed them into the little closet in the sewing room and then went outside.

I headed over to Andy El's and had breakfast with her. She had made oatmeal again, and she gave me a big bowl, sprinkled with cinnamon and brown sugar and lots of milk. She went out to get to the garden before it got too hot, and I got busy getting the stand all set up for the day.

Word had got around the park about the muffins, and they were all sold out by the end of the day. I had also sold two more books and three more jars of Andy El's jam. I had refilled my jug twice since lunchtime, and I was feeling pretty good about things as I headed back to Andy El's to wash the dishes and tidy up for the day.

Andy El was out in the yard doing laundry. She had an old wringer washing machine that she plugged into an extension cord out the window of her trailer and filled up with the hose. When it emptied, she drained it into a huge tin bucket and used that to water her garden.

"It's not good to waste things, Truly," she would tell me. "You gotta think about smart ways to use all you got."

Clarice used to laugh at Andy El for "that ridiculous old dinosaur" of a machine she had, and even though Andy El had offered her the loan of it anytime, Clarice would just take her laundry to Mrs. Bateman's apartment once a week, because her mother would grudgingly let her use the small washer and dryer in her apartment above the store, if it was a small load. Which meant that somehow my stuff never seemed to fit in.

"No way in hell I'm hanging up a bunch of wet clothes," she'd say. "Too much work." And even though she had to suffer through a visit with Mrs. Bateman, she would bundle up all of her laundry and take it over.

There was no laundry service at the trailer park, so most folks went into town to the laundromat.

Andy El, of course, with her trusty old wringer washer, always did her laundry outside, as well as that of her family, even in the winter months. When the rain set in, she would just drag it over into her shed so she'd be out of the rain. She would always let me throw my stuff in with hers, and I would just hang it up on her clothesline. In the winter time, we would have laundry hanging all over inside Andy El's trailer, but, as she said, it got the job done.

I loved to help Andy El run that machine. The motor made a comforting *ka-chug ka-chug ka-chug* sound as the water sloshed inside. The best part was getting to operate the mangle. When the clothes were all washed and rinsed, you carefully fed them through two rollers on top that squeezed out all of the excess water. This made the drying time way shorter for the clothes. You had to be watchful with sheets and other large items, though, because if you didn't guide them carefully enough, they could run too close to the side of the mangle and get covered with grease.

I would always offer to help Andy El, even when she did laundry for Esther and her family, or for Raymond. Andy El would let me run the mangle while she set up extra clotheslines all around her yard, and we would peg out load after load of wash, just laughing and talking.

Andy El loved to tell me stories about when she had been a little girl and had lived in a longhouse on the beach with all of her relatives. The long house was so big that each family had their own section, with their own cooking fire.

I loved to hear the stories about her mother, who seemed to be a lot like Andy El. Andy El told me once that when her mother washed laundry by hand in a big tub, once in a while she would take her big bedsheet and tie it up on a tall pole on her canoe to rig it like a sail. Then they would all set off across the bay to visit with Andy El's auntie and her family for a few days.

"We'd get a real nice visit, and then when we got back home, that sheet was all dry." Andy El would laugh delightedly at how clever her mother had been to find such a useful way to dry her sheet.

When I'd finished the dishes and packed up the jars of jam and the books, I headed out to help Andy El with the laundry.

We laughed and chatted as we hung everything up on the clothesline that Raymond had strung up years before between two trees. Then she invited me in for dinner. Of course, I didn't hesitate. She cooked up some ground beef with onions and lots of fresh vegetables from the garden. It was a real feast. After dinner, we sat out in her yard, and

Andy El knitted while I got a start on another Miss Marple book. I was determined to get better at this detective thing. I couldn't help yawning as the dusk closed in around us. Finally, when it got dark, we headed off to bed. I was asleep as soon as I hit the porch couch.

The next day, I set up the stand and sat reading my latest Miss Marple book.

Mrs. Marshall came out of her trailer and walked over with another cookie tin in her hands.

"Good morning, Truly," she said. "I heard you sold out of the first batch of muffins, so I baked some more for you. This time they're apple cinnamon!"

"Gee, thanks, Mrs. Marshall!" I said gratefully. "Would you like a glass of lemonade on the house in exchange?"

"Oh, heavens no, dear," she replied firmly. "I love to bake, so really you're doing me a favor by selling all these extra muffins for me. I insist on buying a glass. You've got a puppy to save for, after all!" With a smile, she put a dime on the table to pay for her lemonade.

That made a great start to the day. After I made and hung up a new muffin sign for the stand, my sales got pretty brisk.

I seemed to have become a mainstay for the folks in the trailer park, and even Mr. Wyman stopped by like clockwork for a glass of lemonade, and now a muffin every day. I couldn't help feeling proud of this rickety old lemonade stand and all of my hard work. *Maybe Andy El was right*, I thought to myself. *It is important to learn how to earn and save money*. I was starting to feel independent as I added up my money each day, and that was a good feeling. I was starting to realize why she'd wanted me to run the stand.

The day passed quickly and pleasantly. I sat in my chair by the stand, the sun filtering through the cedar branches overhead, and read my Miss Marple book, serving customers as they came and went. And as the day progressed, I couldn't help feeling as though things were going well for me. I figured that I had saved about half of the money that I needed to go to Vancouver for a weekend, stay with Angela, and find my dad.

Andy El had made some chopped egg sandwiches and brought them over to the stand, and we sat together for lunch, washing them down with a glass of lemonade.

She sat and watched me sell a few glasses of lemonade, as well as a jar of jam and two more books to customers who stopped by, and then she commented, "You're doin' a real good job with this stand, Truly. I sure am proud of you. I think you're learning lots about working and earning and saving money." Then she patted me on the arm and added, "I better get back to my garden, and then fold all that laundry." She gathered up our plates and headed back to her trailer.

I couldn't help it: I was filled with pride. I basked in Andy

El's praise for a few moments, and then went back to reading my Miss Marple book.

As far as I could hear, Clarice had been home all day. Her radio had been blaring, and the sound made it all the way up to my stand, so I figured that she must be sewing. Maybe, with any luck, she was working on Elvis's jumpsuit. I hoped that she would get it done quickly, return it to him, and then forget all about him.

By the time I closed up the stand for the day, I decided that I really needed to brace myself for the worst and head to the trailer to see how Clarice was getting on with Elvis's jumpsuit.

First, I washed all of my dishes, and then left the jug and glasses drying in Andy El's dish rack. Then I headed down to the trailer.

When I got to the door, I listened for a moment. I could hear Clarice singing along with the radio. She seemed to be in a good mood, so I opened the door and stepped in. She was sitting at the kitchen table, carefully stitching the lapel by hand. She looked up and said, "Hey, Truly, how's it going? Keepin' outta trouble?"

"I'm okay, Clarice," I answered. "How's the sewing going? Is that Mr. Kingsley's jumpsuit?"

She stretched and said, "Yeah, I'm just about done with it. I just want to get it all done and outta my hair."

I was so relieved to hear her say that that I actually pulled out the chair across from her and sat down.

"It looks really great," I commented.

"Yeah, well, it should. I've been workin' on this all day, and I just want to get it all finished." She tied off the thread and clipped it with her sewing scissors.

"All right, there, it's all done," she said. "So, why don't you go let him know? He can come by anytime to pick it up before I go to work at five."

"Okay, I'll go now," I said, and headed out.

"Tell him he can come by for a drink!" she called after me. Inside, I cringed at her words. Reluctantly, I headed to Elvis's trailer and knocked on his door.

After a moment, he opened it and said, "Well hi there, Truly, how're things?"

"Hello, Mr. Kingsley, Clarice told me to tell you that your jumpsuit is ready."

"Well, that's great, Truly," he said.

Unenthusiastically, I added, "She says you should come by for a drink and pick it up." I could feel my face burning with the shame. I ducked my head down so he wouldn't see.

He was silent for a few moments, and then spoke, slowly. "You know, Truly, I'm awful busy rehearsing and getting ready to perform in the parade. I just don't think I have time for that."

I looked up hopefully as he continued.

"Can you give your mom a message from me? Tell her that's real nice, but I just don't have any spare time, what with rehearsing and all. If she can just let you know what I owe her, maybe you can just deliver the suit back to me. Would that be okay with you?"

"Oh, sure! I'd be happy to do that for you!" I said, and headed back to Clarice's to let her know.

Clarice seemed to be so insulted by Elvis's refusal of her offer of a drink that right then and there she hung the repaired jumpsuit back on the hanger and covered it up with the plastic dry cleaning bag. She angrily grabbed a piece of scrap paper and a pen and wrote out the price on it, and then added: *Just give the money to Truly.*

"Take the damned thing right now, will ya, Truly? I want that jerk's stupid suit outta here!"

Feeling very important, and very relieved, I took it over to Elvis's trailer, holding the garment bag high so the wide bell-bottoms on the white jumpsuit wouldn't drag and get all dusty. With the silver sequins in patterns all down the front and the side of the legs, it was a beautiful, classic Elvis suit. And I had to admit, Clarice had done a great job on the repairs.

I knocked politely on Elvis's trailer and waited as he checked over the repair. I could tell that he was relieved when he saw that it looked good. He got the money, and when he handed it to me, he said, "Thanks, Truly, I sure do appreciate you doing this for me," and then he added, "So, Truly, it's just — you and your mama?" I nodded.

"It's none of my business, but what about your dad?' he asked. I just looked at him, now suddenly worried that he was actually interested in Clarice. But he was looking kindly at me, so I explained how things were.

"I don't know where he is, or who he is." I shrugged. "It's always been just me and Clarice." I thought for a minute and added, "And Andy El, of course! Me and her do lots of stuff together. This summer Andy El helped me get the lemonade stand set up. And she taught me how to make strawberry jam, too."

Elvis was real quiet for a moment, and then he said in the kindest voice I think I had ever heard, "That's real nice of her, doin' things like that for you. You're real lucky to have Andy El in your life."

For some reason, that made me want to cry. I left fast, took the jumpsuit money to Clarice, and then went straight back to Andy El's.

CHAPTER 15

Three days later, it was Friday, and that meant Newman Bay Days were here. Tomorrow there would be a parade, and then right after that the midway would open, with rides and games and cotton candy and all sorts of other treats, all at the large park in town next to the library.

Raymond had walked over to Andy El's through the Cut and offered to take Andy El and me to town to see the parade along with Agnes and Linda. Esther would be working at the café all day.

The twins were excited about us all going together. I agonized for a few minutes, and then said yes. I had been saving so hard and hadn't spent one penny of my money so far this summer. I had counted and re-counted to make sure, and I had earned $10.75. I was nearly halfway to getting to Vancouver. The ferry ticket would cost me $4.00 each way, and then I still had to save for the bus fare and then some food along the way.

But it sounded like so much fun, to go with Agnes and

Linda, and of course Andy El and Raymond. I decided that I could take just one dollar of my hard-earned money and treat myself to a ride on the Ferris wheel or some cotton candy at the fair in the park after the parade. It would just put off my trip another week or so, and that was okay in the long run. I had worked so hard that I figured that I deserved a day off. Besides, I would get to see Elvis perform. I imagined standing with my dad, watching the parade, and seeing how excited he got when Elvis came by on his float. At least if I went to see Elvis perform, I could tell him all about it when I met him in Vancouver.

Raymond headed back home, and Andy El and I got ready for the next day.

As far as Andy El was concerned, Saturday night was always hair washing time, but this week it would be on a Friday night. Andy El let me have a shower in her little bathroom and wash my hair, and then insisted I go get some clean clothes to go to town. She did the same.

I headed back to Clarice's and dug in my dresser for a clean light blue T-shirt and some jean shorts. I would wear them with a pair of runners that I found in the closet. Up till now they had been too big for me, but my feet had grown this summer, and they now fit me. They were white with fancy royal blue stripes on the side. I even found a clean pair of dark blue socks in my drawer, so I didn't need to do any laundry tonight. And for once, everything even matched.

Saturday morning, Andy El and I were up early, washed and ready to go. Andy El packed us a lunch of fry bread and baloney sandwiches, all wrapped up in wax paper. She made a big thermos of tea, so we wouldn't go hungry or thirsty.

Raymond's truck pulled into the driveway, and we climbed in. Andy El got in the front, and I clambered into the back with Linda and Agnes. The three of us laughed and chattered so much we must have sounded like a bunch of ravens as we drove into town.

Boy, was it busy in town! We had about twenty minutes before the parade started, so Raymond parked in the A&P parking lot, and we headed off to find a clear piece of side-walk on Main Street.

I was excited to see the parade this year, but also a bit nervous. I didn't come to town very often, as I never had much money for shopping and therefore not much reason to go. I also felt uncomfortable in town. It may have been simply my imagination, but I always felt that people stared at me and whispered about me behind my back.

I had decided that I would stand with Andy El and the others to watch the parade, and that I wouldn't go and help Mrs. Bateman with the batons this time. I didn't think that she would be any madder at me than she usually was.

In fact, I figured she would probably be relieved to not have me show up. Besides, the girls in the majorette troupe weren't exactly friendly to me. I knew most of them from school, and they all either ignored me or, when they did speak to me, treated me like trash.

This year, I decided, I wanted a chance to actually enjoy the parade with my friends, just like everyone else, and not be made to feel like I was in the way.

I also really wanted to see the town's reaction when Elvis showed up on his float. I wanted to be there when his secret became public and everyone realized that Elvis Presley was alive and well and living in Eagle Shores Trailer Park. I wanted to remember and savor all of the details so I could tell my dad all about it. And I wanted Elvis to know that I had kept his secret, all safe, right till the end for him.

So we all stood, chatting excitedly with the rest of the gathering crowd. And then, just like that, the parade started. First came the police chief, sitting in the squad car with the lights flashing and siren blaring.

Then came the veterans from the Legion in their old war uniforms, marching proudly down the street. Everyone clapped hard for them. It was hard to think those regular-looking old men were true war heroes, but I knew it was so.

"Look, Truly, here comes your grandma's troupe," said Andy El, pointing.

I held my breath as the Newman Bay High Steppers proudly marched around the corner onto Main Street. They really did look fine in their new uniforms, and I had to admit that Clarice had done them proud with all her hard work sewing.

They tossed their batons high in the air, spun themselves around, and then caught them smartly as they marched past us, showing off their precision drills. I knew the lead girl, Natalie, from school. She was a few years older than me and had always been very full of herself, and not particularly kind to me. I had to admit she was really good, though. She blew a whistle, and all of the girls began to march briskly on the spot, their clean white shoes with sparkly red laces stamping in unison. High stepping, they leapt and twirled and sashayed in and out of their choreographed formations, without missing a beat or dropping a baton. They really were good. And then, with another sharp blast of Natalie's whistle, they marched off down the street. Everyone cheered for them and their new routine.

Mrs. Bateman marched alongside them. She was so proud of her troupe: you could tell by the big smile on her face and how her chest was all puffed out. At least, until she caught sight of me. That's when her smile faded, and then she frowned as her eyes swept over Andy El, Raymond, and the twins as they stood beside me. I nearly waved at her, but I decided she wouldn't like that, so I didn't. Besides, she had looked away from us so quickly that she wouldn't have seen it anyway.

There was a lot more in the parade after that: clowns, the high school marching band, lots of floats, and then, at the very end, came the big surprise: Elvis.

I held my breath as the Chamber of Commerce float came around the corner. There he was, Elvis Presley, front and center on the float in his beautiful sequinned costume, playing his guitar and singing away into the microphone, a huge grin on his face. For the entire town to see.

The whole crowd around us gasped, and then cheered and applauded like crazy as he passed slowly by. Elvis caught sight of us, and as his song ended, he struck his famous karate-style pose and pointed right at me. Then, as the crowd went even wilder, Elvis grinned, waved to everyone, and said into the microphone, "Well thank you, folks, thank you very much!" and broke right into "Return to Sender" without skipping a beat.

Now his secret was out.

And I was so proud that everyone knew that I was Elvis's friend. Agnes and Linda were chattering excitedly, and Raymond and Andy El and were laughing and shaking their heads, they were so surprised.

"Well, who woulda guessed?" Andy El said, laughing. "That Aaron Kingsley sure is talented!"

As the parade ended, the crowd broke up, and everyone headed to the park. Andy El told us girls to walk on over with the crowd, and she and Raymond would get our packed lunch and bring it over. We agreed to meet by the stage, where, after some boring speeches and opening ceremonies, there would be entertainment for the rest of the afternoon.

As we walked, Agnes and Linda laughed and chattered about the parade. I walked silently and tried to listen to bits of conversations all around us, to see what people thought about Elvis. I was sure that this was what Miss Marple would have done.

I heard snippets like, "I've never seen an Elvis impersonator before, that sure was great!" And "I've seen that fella around town — who knew he could play the part of Elvis so well!"

I was real confused. I would have thought it was so clear to everyone, just like it was to me. This was the real Elvis Presley. I just couldn't understand why no one else could see it as clearly as I could. Okay, sure, I had heard all about Elvis Presley impersonators, but in the magazines none of them looked and sounded and acted this much like

Elvis Presley. I knew that Aaron Kingsley really was Elvis. The King.

But then it dawned on me — Elvis's secret was still safe! No one else could see the truth about him. They all thought that he had been doing an impersonation of Elvis Presley, and that meant that everything would still be the same at the trailer park. But I knew that it wasn't just an act, that when he got off stage he didn't stop being Elvis. I knew that even at the trailer park, when he was alone singing in his trailer, he wasn't just Aaron Kingsley. He was Elvis.

With that I cheered right up, and as we walked quickly over to the park, I joined in the chatter with the twins.

CHAPTER 16

The twins and I worked our way to the park with the rest of the crowds, and when we got to the stage, we stood looking around.

My heart sank as I saw Natalie and another majorette heading toward us. I could tell they were swaggering a bit to show off their new uniforms, and they were laughing and twirling their batons casually, just to draw attention to themselves. I knew from school how mean they could be.

"Well, if it isn't old Truly," said Natalie. She swished her blond hair from her shoulder and twirled her baton. I hated to admit it to myself, but she did look real pretty in that short, blue majorette skirt with a swirl of sequins running up the side.

"What are you doing with these girls?" said Penny, the other girl. She looked Agnes and Linda up and down, and from the disagreeable expression on her face I could tell that as far as she was concerned, Agnes and Linda were far beneath her. The twins both saw her look, and both of them got silent. They froze and just stared at the ground, looking like they wanted to disappear.

"Don't you know they're — different?" said Natalie, in a condescending voice. "Can't you get any real friends?"

"Yeah," said Penny, "I mean, hanging out with Indians! God, Truly, is that the best you can do?"

I looked at Natalie and Penny, and all they represented: being popular, having a real mom and dad, going to summer camps, taking swimming lessons, living in a real home with a real family. Everything I wished I had. Everything I had been so jealous of on the last day of school, on that bus ride home where I'd listened to them all and felt like such an outsider.

After a few seconds I said thoughtfully, "Yeah, you know, you're right, they sure are different from you two." Natalie and Penny both smirked triumphantly, but then their smiles faded as I added, "Linda and Agnes are both fun to be with, and generous and kind. They don't say mean stuff about people, or give people nasty looks, or worry about what people think. And if those are qualities that you need to have in a friend, well then you can keep yours. I'll just stick to my own, thanks."

Natalie got mad at that, but Penny grabbed her arm and started to pull her away. "Forget about them, Natalie. They're just jealous they can't be majorettes, too."

That's when Elvis walked up, smiling at all of us. He had changed and was now wearing bell-bottom jeans and a studded denim jacket. He still wore a belt with a huge buckle with the initials *TCB* on it, although this one wasn't nearly as big as the one on his costume.

"Hey, Truly, so how was that for a surprise?" He grinned me. Then his smile took in Linda and Agnes as well, and he added, "I gotta say, it sure felt good to look out and see some friendly faces in that crowd! I love to perform, but it sure feels good to have some folks you know out there."

Then he turned to Natalie and Penny, who were smiling eagerly at Elvis. He glanced at their majorette outfits and said, "Take it from me, girls, you're gonna want to get out of those costumes right away. It's easy to get a stain or tear some sequins, and you don't want that to happen."

I smiled to myself as their eager smiles faded.

And then, the bottom dropped out of my stomach. Mrs. Bateman came marching up to our group, and when she saw me, she glared and pinched her nostrils even more than usual.

"Truly, where the dickens were you this morning? The one day a year I actually could use you, and you weren't there to help me out! I had to hand out all of the batons myself, on top of everything else I had to do!"

Her eyes swept over Agnes and Linda, and her mouth went into an even thinner line.

Then she noticed Elvis, looked him up and down, and said, "So you're what all the fuss has been about? Your performance is all everyone's been talking about since the parade ended. It seems it was all anyone saw. Certainly not all the hard work my girls put in this year on their twirling, not the new routines, nor all my efforts."

She glared at him as though he had gone in the parade deliberately to spite her.

Elvis just smiled calmly at her and said, "Oh, you must be Truly's grandmother. I've heard all about you. You must be real proud of this fine girl."

I could see Mrs. Bateman's back get even stiffer. I could tell she was even madder.

And then Elvis added, "From what I saw, your troupe did a real fine job. You got some real talented majorettes there. Of course, no one really appreciates all the hard work and practice that goes into a show."

That seemed to calm her down some, because she could only nod stiffly at Elvis. Then she turned to Natalie and Penny and said, "Now, what the devil are you girls doing still in your costumes! Those are brand new, and I will not allow you to wear them around this dirty old fair. We still have our competitions to think of! Now go get changed at once!"

We watched as Mrs. Bateman marched Natalie and Penny off to get changed. Then Elvis turned to the three of us and said, “How ’bout I treat you girls to some lunch?”

CHAPTER 17

It was the best Newman Bay Days ever for me, and I am sure for Linda and Agnes as well. Elvis bought us each a hot dog, a drink, and then some cotton candy. We all went over to where Andy El and Raymond were sitting on a blanket, and Elvis joined our group, laughing and talking like he was old friends with all of us. He accepted a cup of tea from Raymond's work thermos, and even had a baloney sandwich from Andy El's packed lunch.

Then he insisted on taking us girls over to the midway, and he paid for us to go on the Ferris wheel, and the Tilt-a-Whirl too. We spent the afternoon with him, just laughing and having fun. I had never been on the rides before, because there had never been any extra money for that kind of thing with Clarice, but I tried to act like I had so that Agnes and Linda wouldn't know.

And all throughout the day, people came up and shook Elvis's hand and told him what a great job he'd done and how it'd felt just like watching the real Elvis Presley perform.

He had a little smile on his face, and he kept saying, "Well, thank you, sir. That sure means a lot to me" or "That's real kind of you, ma'am, I'm so glad you enjoyed it."

I felt so proud that Linda and Agnes and I got to walk around with him, enjoying the fair, so that everyone could see that he was our friend. It made me feel kind of special.

Then, when it was all over, the four of us walked back to our meeting place by the stage, where we met up with Raymond and Andy El, who were ready to go home. We thanked Elvis, but he just brushed it off, saying, "You girls just made my day. It sure was worth it!"

He headed off to his Sun Bug, climbed in, and drove off with a wave and an Elvis smile. We all got into Raymond's truck and headed back to Eagle Shores, us girls in the back of the truck, tired but chattering away, reliving every moment of the day.

It was late afternoon when we got home, nearly dinnertime. We were all so worn out from such a big day that Agnes and Linda went home to change into their swimsuits and met me down on the beach for a swim. I just went in the ocean in my cutoffs and T-shirt, since I didn't have a bathing suit. It was such a hot day that the ocean water actually felt warm. When we got out, we dried ourselves on our towels and sat on a huge log, chatting about the day and how much fun we had had.

Then we headed back up to the trailer park and sat around Andy El's back yard to drink the rest of the thermos of tea and eat the leftover baloney sandwiches from our lunch.

I was yawning and could barely stay awake, so after an hour or so I said goodbye, wandered down to Clarice's trailer, and fell asleep on the couch. Aside from Mrs. Bateman and the rude majorettes, it had been a great day.

CHAPTER 18

After Newman Bay Days, the summer fell in to a steady routine. Every morning I would set up my lemonade stand and set out the jug and the glasses, the homemade jam, and the rest of the books for sale. Every few days Mrs. Marshall would come by with a fresh supply of muffins for me to sell, which had become very popular.

I spent my days at the stand reading Miss Marple books, serving my steady stream of customers, and then stopping for a quick lunch midday with Andy El. Evenings we would work in her garden, when it was cooler. I would help her weed and water and pick the vegetables as they ripened. Then we got to work canning or freezing everything for winter.

Clarice was gone most days, off with her boyfriend, and evenings she worked at the tavern. I saw less of her this summer than in past years, but I was so busy with my lemonade stand and saving money that I didn't really notice.

I would casually keep tabs on Elvis, who was out a lot more these days, now that he was known around town as a performer. He got hired to play for the Chamber of Commerce summer barbecue on the August long weekend. There were posters up all over that said: *Elvis Presley Tribute Artist*. Which was apparently the proper way to say Elvis impersonator. He came home afterwards, really pleased with how it had gone. To hear him describe it, they all loved his act. And not one of them suspected that he was the real Elvis Presley.

I still found lots of reasons to casually saunter by his trailer and peer furtively through the living room window or the open door to watch him rehearse. Which he did, faithfully, every day. I guess that was part of being Elvis Presley that he really missed — the performing part. I knew that he loved his new, quiet, private life living at Eagle Shores, though, because whenever he came and went he would be whistling and seemed happy. Maybe living such a quiet life was all he really wanted in the end, and that's why he was hiding out, pretending to be an Elvis impersonator.

Every few days, Agnes and Linda would come over to Andy El's through the Cut and help me at the lemonade stand, followed by a swim in the bay. Those days seemed to go by a lot faster, since having them there with me made it a lot more fun.

On those days, we would walk over to the Wymans' farm and visit the puppies. They were getting bigger each day and were now wandering around and eating mushy food out of a dish, to give Lady a break.

It was really starting to bother me that everyone thought that I was saving for a puppy, when I was really saving to go to Vancouver and find my dad.

One afternoon, as I was cleaning up and putting away the lemonade stand, I made a decision. I would ask Clarice for permission to go to Vancouver by myself to spend a weekend with Angela. I knew that she would say yes. Well, I was pretty sure she would. Clarice was a pretty casual parent, and I didn't think it would bother her to let me go alone on the ferry. I would just leave out the part about meeting my dad. I figured she'd find out soon enough, when I brought him home to meet Elvis. I just had to wait for the right moment to ask her. And then I could start telling people that I had decided to spend my money on a trip to Vancouver to visit Angela. Everyday I would tell myself, *Tomorrow. I'll ask her tomorrow*. And everyday slipped into the next.

Sometimes I would go down to Clarice's trailer and forage for something to eat in the little fridge, but mostly it was empty, since Clarice was home less and less as the summer wore on.

Occasionally she would come home for a change of

clothes or to get a towel to head off to the lake for a swim with her new boyfriend, but that was about it.

I guess things were going well with him, but she still hadn't told him about me. One day our paths crossed. I had gone to rummage around for some clean jeans in my dresser, and she came in.

"Well, hey, Truly, how's it going?" she said, absently, pulling out a towel from the bathroom closet.

"Fine, I guess," I said to her. She was in a pretty good mood. And she appeared to be sober, too.

"So, Clarice, I need to tell you something," I said, trying to sound casual. I decided to tell her that I wanted to go to Vancouver for a weekend and stay with Angela. That way, I could tell Andy El all about it and feel less guilty about not telling her my real plan.

"Yeah, well, make it quick," she said. "Byron's waiting for me to head out to the lake before my shift tonight at the tavern."

"That's his name?" I asked."Byron?"

"Yep," said Clarice. "He's a real great guy, too."

"Have you told him about me yet?" I asked hesitantly.

"Not yet, but I will. Soon." Clarice sounded evasive. "He's not really into kids, but he'll come around." Even she didn't sound too convinced. I decided I'd better change the subject and get brave enough to tell her about my plan to see Angela. But I would leave out the part about meeting my dad.

"I've been earning money this summer, running the lemonade stand," I began. She turned to listen to me, and I could tell she was all of a sudden interested in what I had to say.

"Oh yeah? That's real great, kid. How much ya got saved up?" she asked. There was a funny gleam in her eyes, but I had to keep going to get it all out in a rush.

"I've saved up twenty-four dollars and seventy-five cents," I said proudly.

Clarice sat down at the dinette table and said slowly, "Say, kid, that's really great. Imagine that! You, saving all that money." She sat thinking, and I was just about to blurt out my plan when she suddenly asked, "So, where you got that money? You got it in a real safe place?"

"Oh, sure," I said. "I got it stored in a jar I keep on top of the fridge on Andy El's porch, so it's real safe there."

"Well, that's real fine, real fine," Clarice said. "Listen, I got to go, I'll see ya around in a day or two, kid. Imagine you earning all that money, huh?"

She grabbed an outfit from her closet and headed off in her car, leaving me sitting in the empty trailer. It was only then that I realized that I hadn't had time to ask her about my trip to Vancouver.

CHAPTER 19

One morning I woke up and realized that I had one more day of being eleven. Tomorrow was my twelfth birthday. I grinned to myself and stretched happily. It had been such a great summer so far. And now, I had a birthday.

When I got up, Andy El was already out in her garden, watering and pulling weeds. There was fry bread waiting for me, and a pot of tea beside the jar of jam. I ate, got washed, and went outside.

"Good morning there, sleepyhead." She smiled at me. "I was startin' to wonder if you were ever gonna get up. Or maybe just sleep right on through till you turn twelve!"

"You know it's my birthday tomorrow?" I said in surprise.

"Well, of course I know that," she answered. "Now, I've been thinkin' up a real nice birthday for you."

She paused and then said carefully, "Do you know if your mama will be home some time today?"

I drew a pattern in the dirt with my toe, shrugging. "Not sure. She hasn't said." I tried to sound nonchalant. I hadn't seen Clarice in three days, and that was when she'd driven up in the old beater for what she referred to as a "pit-stop," where she came by to change her clothes for work. Before that, it had been four days since she had been at the trailer.

She seemed to be spending all her time with Byron, and I was starting to get the feeling that she wasn't ever going to tell him about me.

"Well, you leave things up to me, and don't you worry about your birthday." She smiled.

"Thanks, Andy El," I said and threw my arms around her. "I don't want to be a bother, though."

I had never really had a birthday party, or any fuss at all on my birthdays. Clarice would usually forget about my birthday, and if she did remember, it was to give me some half-hearted attempt at a gift.

One year she gave me a used puzzle from a thrift shop with a note taped on the lid that said, "Two pieces missing." Another year she gave me a faded sundress that was way too small.

I had learned early that it was the thought that counted. I knew that in her heart she meant well, but Clarice always had a lot on her plate, her mind was always running in different directions, and she could never remember things like my birthday.

I was always grateful my birthday was in the summer time

so that I didn't have to go to school and explain why I didn't bring in nicely decorated cupcakes like all of the other kids did, or have a special birthday party. Having a birthday in the summer made it easier to forget about it.

Andy El held on tight to me, then she started sniffing like she all of a sudden had a cold, and said, "How could you be a bother to anybody, my Truly girl?"

Then she added, "Now, you get on and get that lemonade stand set up!"

I ran off to make the lemonade and get things set up for the day at our table. She almost made me look forward to this birthday party she was planning. But now that I was going to be twelve, I knew not to have big expectations about things like birthdays. And I knew it was time to get on that ferry and go to Vancouver and find my dad.

CHAPTER 20

The next day I woke up, and couldn't figure out why I was feeling happy. Then I remembered — it was my birthday!

I jumped up off the porch couch and rushed into the trailer.

Andy El was sitting at the kitchen table and said, "Well, good morning, birthday girl!" She got up and gave me a huge hug and a kiss.

I sat down, and at my place at the table was a gift, wrapped in green tissue paper. I stared at it in wonder. A present, a wrapped-up present. For me!

Andy El sat, smiling, and said, "Open it up!" I carefully untaped the paper and slowly unwrapped the parcel, savoring the moment. As I pulled back the paper, I found a beautiful pair of knitted mittens inside. They were thick and knitted in the traditional Salish patterns with brown- and cream-coloured wool.

"Oh, Andy El, they're so beautiful!" I breathed. I tried

them on. They fit perfectly. I jumped up and gave her another hug, with my mittens on.

"'Course, you're gonna have to wait for winter to wear them, but I thought you could use a good pair of mittens this year, to keep you warm," she said, smiling at me.

I couldn't remember ever getting such a wonderful gift. I kept them on my hands and stared at them in wonder.

"Those there," said Andy El, pointing to a line of pattern, "that's waves, on the ocean." She pointed to another geometric design. "That's ivy. Not too much room on mittens, but I got that in!" She laughed, delighted with my happiness.

"I never had anything so nice before," I said, suddenly feeling shy. "This is the best birthday gift ever!"

Andy El just beamed at me and said, "Well, you better take 'em off to eat and then get that lemonade stand set up and going!"

I reluctantly took them off and laid them beside my plate so that I could run my hand over the soft wool and the beautiful patterns. Suddenly I wished it were fall so that I could wear my mittens all day.

Then I jumped up and got to work setting up the stand, making the lemonade, and getting the cups out. I set out the jars of jam and the last of the books, and then sat down to wait. I hoped that Agnes and Linda would come today and keep me company on my birthday.

I glanced down at Clarice's trailer and felt a bit disappointed that I didn't see her car.

Oh, well, I told myself. *Maybe she'll be home later to wish me happy birthday*. Things got busy, and it stayed pretty steady all day. Mrs. Marshall came over with cupcakes instead of muffins, and insisted that I have one that she had decorated with chocolate icing and sprinkles, just for me.

Everyone at the trailer park seemed to know it was my birthday and stopped by for a glass of lemonade and to wish me a happy birthday.

I couldn't help but feel special, even if Clarice hadn't come home yet.

The morning sped by. After a quick lunch at Andy El's, I made a fresh jug of lemonade and headed back out to my stand.

Raymond walked through the Cut, and I could see him helping Andy El, mowing the lawn around her trailer and moving chairs and things out to her backyard. At last, he wiped his brow and came over to my stand with a big smile on his face.

"I hear you got a special day today. Happy birthday, Truly!" he said, and then added, "I think I'll try one of those birthday cupcakes, and since it's your special day, I'd better buy one for you too! And we better have a glass of lemonade to wash it down, too." He insisted on paying me, even though it was to treat me.

"Thank you, Raymond," I said suddenly feeling very shy. "That was really nice of you." And then I hesitantly asked, "Um, you don't know if Agnes and Linda are coming over today, do you?"

Raymond finished off his lemonade, looked off in the distance at the cedar trees that ringed the property, and shrugged, saying, "Well, seems to me those girls have a whole list of chores to do for their mom today. Maybe they'll be over tomorrow or something. Anyways, I gotta get back home myself."

I said goodbye and tried to hide my disappointment. I had hoped that they could be here to share my day with me.

Raymond said, "Well, I'll see you later, Truly," and, with a wave, he headed off back through the Cut.

Just then Mr. Wyman pulled up in his pickup truck and got out with a big grin on his face.

"Well, howdy, Truly!" he said cheerfully. "I came by for my lemonade from the birthday girl!"

I smiled shyly and poured him a glass.

He took a satisfied gulp and then said, "You know, that puppy of yours is pretty near ready to leave his mama. I think you could come and pick him up next week, if you're all ready for him here."

I just stared at him, wide-eyed. I didn't want to tell him today of all days that I wasn't really going to buy the puppy. I hadn't even had a chance to talk to Clarice about my planned trip to Vancouver, and that was getting closer every day.

I hoped she would come home later today, so I could tell her my plan. Maybe, because it was my birthday, she would actually pay attention to me and think my plan to go and visit Angela was a good idea. And give me her permission.

Just then, as Mr. Wyman drove off back to his farm with a wave, Clarice pulled in to Eagle Shores in the old beater. I waved at her, but she drove right on by me at the lemonade stand and skidded to a stop at her trailer.

CHAPTER 21

I took the empty glasses over to Andy El's, and washed them. Then I made another jug of lemonade and put it in the fridge.

I wiped the counter carefully and hung up the tea towel. Taking a deep breath, I decided I would head down to Clarice's trailer, since she hadn't come up to wish me a happy birthday.

I walked slowly, and hung back at the door. I couldn't help feeling a little nervous. Finally, I made myself open the door and step inside the trailer.

"Clarice?" I called. I could hear her in her bedroom, and I headed down the hall to find her.

She had a battered old blue suitcase out on the bed and was quickly pulling piles of clothes out of her dresser drawers and shoving things into the suitcase.

"Oh, hey there, Truly," she said in a real friendly voice. She straightened up and stood in front of the suitcase. "How's the lemonade business?"

"Good. Real good," I said. I waited for her to wish me happy birthday, but after a minute, I could tell she hadn't remembered.

"So, I have this idea that I can do with all my money I've been saving," I started to tell her, but right then she interrupted me.

"Say, kid, how much have you got all saved up?" she asked.

I felt a bit reluctant to tell her, but since she knew that I was saving money, I had to answer. "Well, as of last night, I have twenty-eight dollars and eighty cents all saved up. Today there'll be more, but I still have to pay Andy El for the lemonade and the jam too, so I'm not sure what the new total is."

She smiled eagerly at me and said, "Well, that's just great, Truly, really great. You should, um, bring it on over here to our trailer for safe-keeping."

My heart sank. I knew my money was safe where it was, and it wouldn't be safe with Clarice around. I thought fast to change the subject.

"So, you know what today is, right?" I said brightly.

Clarice sat down on the bed, trying to think. Then I guess it dawned on her that it was my birthday.

"Oh, right," she said. "Wow! That sure snuck up fast, didn't it? You're what — ten? Eleven now?"

"I'm twelve!" I said.

"Holy smokes!" she said. "I have a twelve-year-old kid! Ain't that somethin'!" She shook her head in wonder. "Well, so, you having a good day an' all, I hope?" she added.

I shrugged, trying not to let her know that I was hurt. She would take it personally and get mad at me, and then end up crying about how lousy her life was. Because of me.

"I guess," I said, non-committally. "It's no big deal. It's just a birthday."

"That's the way to look at it!" she said, looking around the room, already distracted.

It was time. I had to tell her about my trip to Vancouver. I took a deep breath and said all in a rush, "So, I've been saving all my money, and I have enough to go to Vancouver on the bus and the ferry and visit Angela. She told me I could when she left. She gave me her address and invited me for a weekend, and I thought that with the money that I saved, I could go over and see her." I looked at Clarice nervously, waiting for her reaction.

"You?" Clarice looked surprised, and then laughed. "Going all the way to Vancouver by yourself? On the ferry?"

I just plowed ahead and kept talking. I had to convince her it was a great idea.

"It would be so nice to see her again, and she invited me. I could spend the weekend with her, like she offered."

My voice trailed off, and I looked uncertainly at her.

She sat there, thinking. And then she surprised me.

"Well, say, kiddo, I think that's a real good idea!" she said. "I think you should go see Angela. You can get the bus on the highway, and it takes you right to the ferry. You still got her address?"

"Really?" I couldn't believe it was going to be this easy. Here I had worried and agonized over just how I could bring up the subject of getting permission to go to Vancouver from Clarice, and I had convinced myself that she would get angry at me for even thinking of it.

"I can really go?" I could barely believe that it was just this easy.

"Well, sure, kid, go ahead, maybe next weekend, okay?" Clarice said. I couldn't believe how nice she was being about the whole thing.

"Be real nice for you to see Angela after all this time," she added.

I stood there, grinning like an idiot I was so happy. "Oh, thanks! Clarice, you won't regret this!" I knew I was babbling, but I couldn't help it. "I'll be really responsible traveling, and a really polite guest when I get there to see Angela!"

She just laughed as she slammed the lid on the suitcase. She straightened up and grabbed her purse and the case. She said, "Well sure, kid, I'll bet you'll have a great weekend with her," and then she headed past me with the suitcase and added, "Well, I gotta go, kid. I'll see ya later, Truly. I'll be home, maybe later, yeah, I should be home later for a while, or tomorrow. Definitely tomorrow. We'll talk more about it then, okay?"

I nodded, grinning at her. She swept by me and headed out to her car, so I followed after her.

I stood in the doorway of the trailer and watched as she loaded her bags into the car and waved to her as she drove off with a careless flap of her hand out the window.

It was only as her car pulled out from Eagle Shores onto the road that it occurred to me that she had forgotten to wish me a happy birthday.

CHAPTER 22

I didn't care. I honestly don't remember whether Clarice had ever wished me a happy birthday. In fact, when I was little I thought that only some people had birthdays, and I was someone who didn't get one.

Because while Clarice always seemed to find a way to celebrate hers, I don't remember having a birthday celebrated for me. I do remember the day I turned five, because Clarice got drunk, slumped on the couch, cried, and kept saying, "Five years ago today my whole life changed. I can't believe it. Five whole years." Even then, it seemed to be more about her getting sad than a day for me to celebrate.

But all that didn't matter anymore — she had said yes to my trip to Vancouver! And that was more important to me than anything. Now I could tell Andy El, and even Elvis.

As I headed back to my lemonade stand, I noticed Elvis was watching from his trailer door.

"Hey, Truly," he said to me as I passed by. "Your mama

goin' away somewhere?" I must have looked surprised, as I thought for a moment.

"Oh, gee," I said. "She didn't actually say. I guess she did have those suitcases with her, didn't she?" Then I shrugged. "She's been staying a lot with Byron, her boyfriend, so I guess she just needed a lot of clothes and stuff over there."

"But is she comin' back to be with you on your birthday?' he persisted.

"I think so," I said slowly. "She said that she might be back later, so I guess so." Clarice hadn't really said if she would be back or not today for my birthday. In fact, she'd been pretty vague.

But more important than having Clarice come home for my birthday was the big news that she had said yes to me going to Vancouver.

With that I ran back to my stand. I didn't look back, but I could feel his eyes watching me all the way. I could tell that he felt bad that Clarice had gone out. But I didn't care. Clarice had said yes to my trip.

Never mind, I thought to myself. *When I bring my dad home, everyone will be so surprised. It will be worth all of this keeping such a big secret. Even if I do feel so darned guilty now.*

CHAPTER 23

The day flew by, and I couldn't help feeling happy. It was really happening! Clarice was okay with me going to Vancouver by myself! I would be able to leave a note for Andy El, and it would be okay.

All afternoon, people kept coming and going to and from my stand, keeping me busy. I was surprised how many people from the trailer park came back for a second glass of lemonade, just to wish me another happy birthday. It really kept me hopping. I had to refill my jug three times after lunch.

And then, finally, Andy El came over about five o'clock and told me it was time to shut down the stand, as she had another surprise for me.

I don't think I'd ever packed up that stand as fast as I did then. When I had washed the jug and all of the glasses, put the jam away on the porch table, returned the now-empty cupcake tin to Mrs. Marshall, and put the tablecloth away, I washed my face and hands at Andy El's. I looked into the mirror at my reflection and inspected my face. I didn't look any different than yesterday.

"I can go to Vancouver and find my dad, and I don't have to sneak away," I whispered to my image, and I grinned at myself.

I smoothed my hair down and straightened my shirt. I was ready for my surprise.

Andy El tied a scarf around my eyes to blindfold me, and then she carefully led me down the steps and outside her trailer, around to the back yard.

"Okay now, Truly, you get ready!" she said, and she untied the scarf. I looked around in surprise.

There, hidden behind the back of the trailer so I hadn't seen from my lemonade stand, was a fire pit all laid out with rocks around it. All Andy El's kitchen chairs were out in a ring around it, and there were other some chairs that I didn't recognize.

There was a bouquet of flowers on the worktable, and I recognized some of Mrs. Williams's roses.

"Oh," I breathed. "Oh," was all I could say.

"We're havin' a party, Truly! For you!" Andy El said proudly. "Me and Raymond set this all up today. Raymond will be back, and Esther, and Agnes and Linda, and Mrs. Williams and Mrs. Marshall. We're gonna have hot dogs, and Mrs. Williams is bringin' potato salad, Mrs. Marshall is bringin' some homemade pickles, and Esther and the girls, they spent today makin' you a birthday cake!"

I couldn't help it. I started to cry. I just hung on to Andy El and sobbed like an idiot. And all I could say was,"Oh, Andy El . . ." over and over again.

No one had ever done anything like this for me before. Not that I could remember, anyway.

Andy El just kept patting me on the back, saying, "Oh Truly, my Truly," over and over again.

And then she finally said, "Enough of that crying, girl! All right now, go wash that face again and come back with a party face on! Everybody'll be here soon!"

I ran in to Andy El's to wash and to find some clean clothes to put on. I felt almost giddy. When I came back outside, I could see that Raymond had driven Esther and the girls over. They were getting out of the truck, and Esther was carefully carrying a plate with a big chocolate cake on it, with icing and candles all ready to light.

I suddenly felt real shy, but when Agnes and Linda raced over and yelled, "Happy birthday, Truly!" and "Surprise!" I couldn't help but start to grin like an idiot again.

Esther put the cake down on the table and gave me a big hug. "Happy birthday, Truly!" she said, smiling.

Even Raymond gave me a quick hug and, with a grin, said, "Happy birthday! I sure hope you were surprised, Truly.

Andy El's been making us work like the dickens to get this all ready for you!"

Mrs. Williams arrived with a big bowl of potato salad, and Mrs. Marshall came over with a plate of pickles. Raymond started sharpening the ends of the long branches he had cut for hot dog sticks, while Andy El lit the fire in the new fire pit.

And so, I had my very first birthday party ever. We laughed and cooked and ate hot dogs, potato salad, and homemade pickles.

And just when I thought it couldn't get any better, Elvis arrived. With a big tub of ice cream for everybody. And he brought his guitar.

"It's Neapolitan ice cream," he explained. "I didn't know what your favorite flavor was, so this way you can have all three: vanilla, chocolate, and strawberry!"

"I don't know what my favorite flavor is either!" I blurted out, and we all laughed.

"Looks like you got the right one, then, Aaron," said Raymond.

CHAPTER 24

And then it was time for my birthday cake. I watched wide-eyed as Esther lit the candles, and Agnes and Linda together carefully carried the cake over to where I sat, with everyone singing "Happy Birthday." I ducked my head shyly, my heart full to bursting.

"Make a wish!" said Agnes and Linda, and I thought hard. It seemed so important that I make the right wish.

I closed my eyes tightly. *Please let me find my dad*, I wished. *Let him be happy to meet me, too!*

Then everyone cheered and clapped as I blew out the candles. Esther and Andy El served up the cake and put ice cream on everyone's plates, and the twins carefully handed out the plates to each person.

I took a bite of Esther's cake, and then a mouthful of Elvis's ice cream. It was the best cake and ice cream I had ever had.

In the evening light, I looked around at everyone at the party — my party. I couldn't ever remember feeling so happy.

When everyone had eaten their cake, Elvis quietly opened his guitar case and took out his guitar.

He stood up and said, smiling right at me, "In honor of your birthday, I thought I would give you your very own special concert, Truly."

I was speechless. And then he started to play and sing. Just for me. Every song he'd made famous, from "Blue Suede Shoes" to "All Shook Up," and then more.

Everyone cheered and clapped after each song, and yelled for more. It was wonderful.

Until Clarice drove up in her old beater.

Her car careened off the road and then lurched to a stop beside Andy El's trailer. The driver's door opened, and she fell out, giggling. She staggered to her feet, looked around, and yelled, "Hey, Truly, where the heck are ya?" and then she started laughing, almost hysterically.

We all sat in shock, listening to her. I was frozen to the kitchen chair that I sat on, and I couldn't move. Even though I knew I should rush over to her and try and to stop her drunken yelling. Even though she was humiliating me in front of everyone. I couldn't seem to make myself move.

She staggered into Andy El's porch, and I heard the sound of glass smashing, then another bang, and then her laughing hysterically again.

Andy El sighed and pulled herself to her feet. "I'm gonna have a talk with her," she said. "Everybody stay here and enjoy this party."

"No, Mama," said Raymond quietly. "I think it's time I had a talk with Clarice about the way things have been going."

Raymond stood up, and that's when Clarice came stumbling into view. She stopped, weaving, and stared when she saw us all sitting around the campfire having a party here at Andy El's. Then she threw her head back and started to laugh. She leaned forward and slapped her knee, and said, "Well, whattya know! There's a party going on! How come you didn't invite me?"

Raymond strode over to her, took her firmly by the arm, and said, "Clarice, I think you need to settle down" in his calm but firm voice.

But Clarice shook off his arm and said, "Hey! Nobody loves a party like I do! I wanna stay!" And then she looked around at us all and said the most horrible thing she could say: "So, what's the special occasion?"

I felt my heart exploding in my chest. I felt hot tears roll down my cheeks. Clarice had already forgotten that it was my birthday.

Esther stood up so fast her chair fell backwards behind her. She looked angry, so angry that I felt a bit afraid. "It's your child's birthday party," she said coldly. "And though it was nice of you to finally show up, I think maybe you're in no fit state to stay here."

I closed my eyes and began to rock back and forth, wishing Clarice would get swallowed up by the darkness.

"Truly's birthday? Well, son of a gun," said Clarice. She sounded surprised, and a bit confused.

Esther crossed over to her, and she and Raymond took Clarice's arms firmly.

"We're going down to your trailer. I want to talk to you," Raymond said, angrily. "And then you're gonna lie down for a while."

Clarice glared at him defiantly, and then looked around the fire at all of us sitting there.

"Well, go ahead, have a party without me!" she said bitterly. "I don't need you people to have fun! I got plans, big plans, anyway. You'll see!"

And the three of them disappeared into the dark. But she didn't get swallowed up. I could hear Clarice objecting loudly all the way. We all could.

Finally, we heard Esther say in an exasperated voice, "That's enough, now put a sock in it, Clarice." She sounded so angry. Raymond must have shut the door after they went into the trailer, because we could no longer hear Clarice yelling at them.

We all sat in shock, no one knowing what to say.

But Elvis knew just what to do. After a few moments, he picked up his guitar again and began to sing "Love Me Tender" in a really gentle voice. It was so beautiful. It was such a pretty song, and so sad-sounding that more tears began to roll down my cheeks. I was grateful that it was dark, and no one could see my face.

And you know what? Andy El started to sing along, too. And Mrs. Williams joined in. And then the twins, and even I did. We just couldn't help but feel the sadness and the beauty in the words, and somehow, it helped make things right.

When we all finished, we just sat for a few moments, letting the song linger right there with us in the summer night.

And then Elvis played "Peace in the Valley" and I think we all felt even better then. I stopped worrying about what was happening with Clarice and Raymond and Esther.

All the while they were down in Clarice's trailer, Elvis just kept on playing and singing. I swear he played every song that he knew. For fun, he even played a few Beatles songs. We all sang along with those, too. After a while, I was able to have some fun again.

Until Raymond and Esther walked back up into the firelight, and I froze up inside again.

Raymond came over and knelt down in front of me

and said in a real kind voice, "Truly, your mama has some things she needs to work out. She's real sorry that she couldn't make your party, and I hope you won't let this ruin your birthday."

Esther just leaned over my chair and hugged me real tight.

Andy El said kindly, "Clarice has some problems, Truly. It doesn't mean she doesn't love you. She just has gotten herself kind of lost, honey. We all love you so very much."

I couldn't bear the idea that they all felt so bad for me.

"It's okay," I said, finally. "This might not sound right, but honestly, I'm glad she couldn't make my party. I know that must sound horrible, but somehow, somehow she'd make it all about her, and not me."

That's when Elvis busted out with "Don't Be Cruel." I couldn't help it. I started to laugh. We all did. And we kept laughing, and singing along with Elvis, well into the night. Elvis had saved my first ever birthday party. As much as my heart was breaking, I was filled with gratitude.

CHAPTER 25

Next morning, I woke up late. Andy El had said I could sleep in and have a late start to the lemonade stand, so I just lay on her couch, with the late morning sun filtering in the curtained window, creating a trail of flower shadows throughout the porch.

Stretching my arms over my head, I smiled to myself while remembering all the wonderful parts of my birthday party. It had been such a special night until Clarice showed up so drunk.

But even with all of that, Raymond and Esther had made her go down to her trailer and go to bed, and then they came back, and then Elvis sang again and made everything okay again.

And what a gift Elvis had given me! My very own special Elvis Presley concert for all of my friends. I would never, ever forget that very special birthday present from him.

And now that Clarice had given me permission to go to Vancouver on my own, I could tell Andy El and go this coming weekend. In two days, I would be on my way to meet my dad and tell him that Elvis Presley was here at Eagle Shores.

I finally got up and went into Andy El's little kitchen. She was sitting at the table with a cup of tea growing cold in front of her.

"Good morning," I said. "I guess I slept in. But I'll get the stand set up real fast, I promise, Andy El!" I said as I sat down and reached for a piece of fry bread.

Andy El waited until I had a piece covered in jam and had taken a few bites. Then she said quietly, "Truly, I gotta tell you something, something real important."

There was something in her voice that made me stop chewing and put down my bread. It was suddenly hard to swallow. I sat, stilled, and waited, now worried.

"Clarice is gone," she said quietly.

"Oh, really?" I said. That was nothing; Clarice was always gone these days. She was probably off somewhere with Byron, at the lake or something. I felt relieved that I didn't have to see her so soon after my party. Because if she remembered anything about it, somehow she would make it all my fault that she had acted so badly.

"No, Truly, I mean really gone." Andy El looked sad. "She packed most of her things up and took them, and she left a note for you."

I just stared at her, not understanding.

Andy El sighed.

"I went down there this morning, to try and talk to her. I try not to interfere with Clarice, I figure she's gotta find her own way, but after last night — well, that was enough for me," she said. "I needed to tell her what I thought of her behavior, last night and all the time. The way she treats you. It's just not right." Andy El shook her head angrily. Then she continued.

"But her car was gone. I went in to check the trailer, 'cause I had a funny feeling, and found this on the table."

She passed me the note. Clarice had written it in green pencil crayon, scrawling the words across a lined sheet torn out of one of my old school notebooks.

It read:

Truly — I got my big break! Byron got me a great job in Vancouver, so I am heading off to the mainland. I'm gonna be dancing in a nightclub, so I won't be able to have you there with me. You stick with Andy El, and I figure she'll keep on lookin' after you. I'll send ya a postcard from the big smoke! See ya around, kid.

Clarice

And that was it. That was goodbye from my mother. She was gone.

I just sat and stared at the paper, and then looked up at Andy El. It wouldn't sink in. It didn't feel real.

Then I stood up and said calmly, "I'm sure it's just a joke. Clarice wouldn't just disappear like that." Then I said, trying to sound cheerful, "Well, I better get that lemonade stand going, or people will think I retired or something!"

I headed back out to the porch to get a can of lemonade out of the freezer. That's when I saw it. The glittering shards of the smashed mason jar in the corner, the jar I had hidden at Andy El's so it was safe. The jar where I had been keeping all the lemonade stand money. Saving and counting over and over again, to make sure I had enough to go to Vancouver and find my dad.

I stood frozen and just stared at the shattered jar. And remembered back to last night, hearing that crash as Clarice stumbled around Andy El's porch.

All of my money was gone.

Finally, in a small voice, I said, "Andy El? She took all my money. All my lemonade stand money. What do I do now?"

I couldn't help it: a tear escaped from my eye and slid down my cheek.

Andy El got up and came over to me and grabbed me in a real tight hug. I started to shake. And sob real hard. Andy El just hung on real tight to me, saying over and over again,

"Don't you worry, Andy El will take care of you. Don't you worry 'bout nothing. I'm here. I'm here."

But even with my eyes squeezed shut, all I could see were the empty, broken shards of the money jar. Now there was no way I would ever get to Vancouver and find my dad.

CHAPTER 26

I don't remember much else about that day. I know that I went down to our trailer and walked through all of the cramped little rooms. Looking for a clue that Clarice would be back.

She had left a lot of her stuff, but she had taken most of her clothes. All of her make-up was gone.

The trailer was in complete shambles. She had obviously just pulled things out of drawers and the closet, tossed onto the bed what she didn't want to take, and then walked out. The radio on her nightstand was still playing, as if she had just stepped outside for a moment. I could still smell her lingering cigarette smoke and her cheap perfume.

In the living room, there were still sequins and bits of thread scrunched into the worn carpet from sewing the majorette costumes. She never was very good at cleaning, and I had been too busy with my lemonade stand to attempt tidying up. I pushed some rejected clothes aside and sat down on the couch, rocking back and forth.

Andy El finally came down to Clarice's trailer to find me. I was sitting on the couch, just sitting and staring at the rug. Later, she told me that I had been down there for at least three hours.

She called me gently, but I didn't answer her. She came over, sat down next to me, and took both my hands in hers.

"Truly," she said. I couldn't look her in the eye.

"I have to wait here," I said to the carpet. "Clarice will be back. You'll see. She'll come back for me. She'll have my lemonade stand money all safe and sound, I know she will."

That's when Andy El put her hands on either side of my face and made me look right at her.

"Truly, it's time to go," she said softly. "We gotta go now." I think I nodded. She took me by the hand and led me out of the trailer and all the way up to her place.

When we got to the door of her trailer, I said dully, "I want to lie down. I need to sleep," and I headed for the old couch on the porch.

That's when Andy El stopped me.

"No, Truly, you stop. I don't want you sleepin' on my porch anymore." I turned and just stared at her in horror. I started to shake all over again. First Clarice had left me, and I would never find my dad. And now, even worse, Andy El was abandoning me.

"You come with me, Truly," she said, and she led me into

her trailer, down the hall past her little bedroom. To her extra bedroom at the end of the hall.

She stopped in the doorway and said, “Look, Truly.” I looked in and saw the bed, nicely made up with a pretty, blue-flowered quilt on it. Pattycake lay on top, her head on the pillow. Under the window there was a small dresser, and on the top was a neatly folded pile of my clothes that Andy El had washed and hung out to dry the other day. I had meant to take them back to Clarice’s, but I had been too busy to get to it.

“You’re gonna stay here with me, Truly,” she said softly. “Properly. This is gonna be your bedroom from now on. No more sleepin’ on the porch. You got your own room, now.”

I collapsed in her arms then, and sobbed. She held me and rocked me, and then got me to lie down on the bed. My bed. She covered me with the quilt, gave me Pattycake to cling to, and told me to sleep. As I drifted off, I hoped that it was true. That I could really stay here with Andy El, and for once, everything would be all right.

I slept.

CHAPTER 27

When I awoke, it was late in the afternoon. I could hear voices in Andy El's kitchen. I listened. I could hear Esther, and then Raymond, talking quietly with Andy El.

"I cannot believe that Mrs. Bateman!" said Esther angrily. Andy El shushed her and told her to keep her voice down so she didn't wake me.

"What did she say?" asked Raymond softly.

"I phoned her, first thing this morning when Mama told me about the note she found, and I told her what that damned Clarice had done, gone and abandoned Truly," said Esther. "She told me that she wasn't surprised, the way Clarice has been carrying on. So I asked her what she planned to do about Truly, and that old witch said she wouldn't do a damned thing for that child! She said she didn't want anything to do with her! Her own granddaughter!"

Raymond sighed. "No wonder Clarice turned out the way she did," he said. "That woman always was such a mean old biddy."

"But that doesn't excuse what Clarice has done!" objected Esther. "I also found out that she quit her job at the tavern two days ago, and one of the girls that works there says that Clarice really has gone to Vancouver with this Byron."

Then Andy El spoke. "Well, I've decided. Truly is gonna stay here with me," she said firmly. "It's like she's my own little girl, anyway," she added. "It won't be nothin' new to have her here permanently."

Esther sighed. "Mama, I know how you feel, and I want that too, but you know they'll never let you keep her."

"Just let 'em try to take her from me!" declared Andy El.

"I just don't know if Social Services will let you keep her, Mama," said Raymond. "She's considered a white girl, after all."

I couldn't bear it any longer. I got up and came out to the kitchen where they were all gathered at the table.

I knew my hair was all tangled up, I was shaking, I felt weak, and my eyes were all puffy. I didn't care.

They all stared at me, and I said, "I think I should go tell the Wymans that they won't need to hold the puppy for me anymore. They can sell him to somebody else now."

"Oh, Truly," said Andy El, her voice breaking.

"It's okay, Andy El," I said. "I wasn't really going to buy the puppy anyway. I was saving to go to Vancouver and see Angela and find my dad. But now I'll never find him."

That's when my knees gave out and I guess I fainted. The whole trailer went black, and I could hear Raymond's voice, as if he was far away down a tunnel: "Mama's right, Esther. Truly's gonna stay right here. Right here with her family."

CHAPTER 28

Later on, I woke up in my bed again. I looked around and saw Andy El sitting in the chair next to the bed, knitting. In the lamp-light, she looked drawn and worried.

"Andy El?" I said in a quiet voice. She looked up and smiled at me, but her eyes seemed so sad that it broke my heart all over again.

"How you feelin', Truly girl?" she asked me. She put down her knitting and came and sat on the edge of the bed, taking my hand in hers. She brushed my hair back off my face with her hand and smiled down at me.

"I guess I'm okay," I said in a small voice. But I wasn't. I felt like I was disappearing.

"Truly, what did you mean about going to Vancouver to find your dad? Whatever gave you that idea?" Andy El asked me kindly, her eyes troubled.

"Angela sent a postcard, and Clarice threw it out. But I found it," I said. "Angela wrote that she saw my dad. So she knows where he is. I wanted to go and find him. And maybe he'd want to come back and be with us — me. And I'd have a real family for once." I couldn't help it, my lip trembled.

Andy El gathered me up in her arms and rocked me, saying, "Oh, you poor, poor, girl. Truly, you got a family already, right here, don't you see that?" Then she sighed. "I am so sorry that things have been so hard for you, Truly, that you would think of doing such a foolish thing."

She paused and looked at me. "You feeling hungry?" she asked. "Esther brought over some homemade soup." I shook my head and turned away to face the wall.

All I could think was that with my money all gone, all my plans were gone too. I remembered that cute little puppy washing my face and wiggling in my arms as I sat in the straw in the Wymans' barn. Even though I hadn't really planned on buying him, I had secretly hoped that when I brought my dad back, he would buy the puppy for me. I couldn't bear to think that my puppy would be going home with someone else. He would never be mine. And now I had no money to go to Vancouver. Now I would never find my dad.

"She took all my lemonade stand money," I whispered, and a tear leaked out of my eye. I didn't think I had any more tears left in me, but I did. I sobbed again in Andy El's arms.

"There, there, Truly girl, don't you worry. Everything's gonna be okay," she said, over and over again. I wished I could believe her.

CHAPTER 29

Later, after I'd finally cried myself out, Andy El insisted that I get up, wash my face, and have some soup. I didn't think that I was hungry, but when I started in on Esther's soup, I realized that I was starving.

As I was finishing, there was a soft knock on the trailer door. Andy El went to answer it. I said in a stricken voice, "I don't want to see anyone, Andy El!"

But as she opened the door, she said, "Oh, my!" and then she said, "Truly, you better come on out here — there's something you need to see!"

Clarice! She's come back! I thought. I jumped up and rushed to the door, and then stopped, confused.

There, in the doorway, stood Elvis, smiling shyly.

"Hey there, Truly," he said. "If you don't mind comin' outside here, there's something you need to see."

I followed Andy El out onto the little patch of lawn. There stood the little brown puppy, straining on a leash, tumbling over his tail, yapping excitedly.

"Oh," I breathed. "The puppy!"

I rushed forward, sat down, and buried my head against the puppy's squiggling body. Elvis put the leash in my hand and said, "Well, here you go, Truly, a late birthday present for you!"

I hugged the puppy close, and then looked up at Elvis and Andy El in wonder.

"But — but — I don't understand," I said.

Elvis grinned at me. "Well, I decided to head on over to the Wymans' and see those puppies you been tellin' me about," he explained. "And I picked up this little fella, and he started following me home, like he was ready to come home to you."

He continued, "So I offered to pay Mr. Wyman for him so you could still get your puppy. But he told me that they were never goin' to charge you for this little guy anyway. They were so impressed with how hard you worked, and how you had saved all your lemonade stand money toward the puppy, they just knew that you'd be a really great dog owner, and that's all they cared about. And Mrs. Wyman told me to bring him on home to you."

"The puppy, Andy El! He's mine!" was all I could say, over and over again.

CHAPTER 30

Within a few days, I started to feel as though it was really going to be okay. I had moved all of my clothes up from the trailer and settled in to Andy El's second bedroom, and I had started to believe that I would be able to go on without Clarice and live with Andy El permanently. Andy El and I had cleaned up Clarice's trailer, emptied out the fridge, and shut things up for now. Until we found out exactly what Clarice's plans were.

I was too shy to start up the lemonade stand again, though. I didn't want to talk to Mrs. Williams or anyone else who might stop in and ask how things were going. I just didn't want to be the center of attention.

Andy El and I had been out picking blackberries for jam that morning. We had stopped for lunch, and I was sitting outside, playing with my puppy. Andy El was out back, rinsing the berries through a strainer, getting ready to make a big pot of jam.

That's when a big beige car drove up, bumping slowly

to a stop beside Andy El's trailer. Out stepped a middle-aged white woman, wearing a beige pantsuit, her hair pulled back into a severe bun. She pulled a briefcase out of her car and headed for the trailer door.

She stepped up and knocked on Andy El's door.

I came up behind her and said, uncertainly, "Can I help you?"

She turned and looked at me and said, "Oh! Oh my, um, you must be Truly." We stared at each other for a few minutes, and then she forced a smile. Unable to do the same, I just kept staring at her with a stricken look on my face.

"I am looking for Ella Charlie. Is this her trailer?" the woman asked in a bright voice.

I nodded. "She's out back," I said in a small voice. "I'll get her."

I ran around the trailer and said urgently, "Andy El! There's a lady here! I think it's about me!" I was trying not to sound scared.

Andy El just closed her eyes for a moment, then opened them. She smiled and nodded at me, handed me the hose, and said, "It's okay, Truly, we'll get this sorted out now, don't you worry."

She dried her hands on her tea towel, and marched around the trailer to where the lady was waiting. I followed behind her.

"I'm Ella Charlie," she said. "What can I help you with?" The lady looked at me, then back to Andy El.

"My name is Nancy Carlisle. I work for Social Services. I need to talk to you about a report of an abandoned child named Truly Bateman. Is there somewhere we can talk?" she asked, and then added, "Privately?"

Andy El nodded at her, and then said to me, "Truly, you see to the rest of those berries. I want you to wait outside while this lady and me talk things over." Then she said to Mrs. Carlisle, "You come on inside, you can wait while I phone my son. He's home today from work. I want him to be here for this conversation." And they disappeared into the trailer.

I stood frozen on the spot, the hose still in my hand, water running into the grass.

From inside the trailer I could hear Andy El on the phone, saying, "I need you here right now, son. A lady's come about my Truly girl. You get here quick."

And then, in less than a minute, Raymond's truck skidded into the driveway and pulled to a stop. He jumped out, slammed the driver's door, and headed straight into the trailer, shutting that door firmly behind him.

I turned off the hose and crept closer to the trailer, holding on to the puppy's leash, shushing him, until I was just by the open living room window. I was terrified, but I needed to hear what was going on.

"My name is Nancy Carlisle, and I am from Social Services," the woman began again. "We had a call from a Mrs. Bateman that you have a young girl living here, and she believes the child should be placed in foster care. She reported that the child had been abandoned by her mother."

I sat down with a thump on the grass, my heart pounding. The puppy crawled delightedly onto my lap.

I heard Andy El's voice as she said calmly, "No. That girl belongs here, with me."

"Mrs. Charlie, you don't seem to understand," said the woman. "Mrs. Bateman is the child's grandmother, and she has called our office to report that the child has been abandoned by the mother, and further stated that as the grandmother, she is unable to take on the raising of Truly, and further stated that she wanted the child to be placed in the Ministry's care."

"That Mrs. Bateman," spat Andy El. "So, she never even offered to take Truly in? Or help out in any way?" There was silence, and Andy El continued, "Well, that don't surprise me none. That woman has done nothing for Truly — ever! Other than been mean and unkind to that child."

"You don't understand how things work, Mrs. Charlie," protested the woman. "She is legally the grandmother, and as her daughter, Clarice Bateman, has abandoned Truly,

Mrs. Bateman has the legal right to have Truly put into care."

"No, you don't understand!" said Andy El. I had never heard her so angry. "I been looking after that child like she was my own since she and that poor excuse of a mother came to my trailer park! And I plan to keep on doin' that for a long time to come!"

"Mama," cautioned Raymond, "take it easy."

"I been feeding that girl and giving her a place to sleep, a place of safety when her mama just left her for days on end, or was too blasted drunk to know what she was doin'!"

I had never heard Andy El raise her voice.

"Mrs. Charlie, I understand —," the woman protested.

"No, Mrs. Carlisle, you don't understand anything, or you'd know what's right for that girl!" yelled Andy El. "She needs to know she's safe, and loved. She needs to know that something will work out okay for her, just once in her life. And she'll get all that stayin' right here with me!"

Mrs. Carlisle sighed. "May I speak to Truly, please?" There was silence, and then she said, "If I can speak to Truly, and have her assurance that she feels safe here, then I am prepared to leave Truly here for a few more days. At this point, I am trying to track down her father, to see if he would be willing to take Truly in. Given some more time, I hope to find him. He may be willing to take full custody of Truly."

"Wait! Her father?" said Raymond. "Are you telling me that Truly's father could get full custody of her? If he wanted to take her in?"

"Well, of course, if he passes our scrutiny," said the woman. "If he can provide Truly with a proper home, and has a good job, then yes. Family is always the best option for a child in this situation."

There was a long silence. I took a deep breath, stood up carefully, and peeked in the window. My heart was pounding. If only I could make my legs move, I could go in and tell them that I knew where my father was. Maybe it wasn't too late to find him and get him to come back.

I could see Raymond and Andy El staring at each other. It was strange, as though in their silence, they were having a whole conversation with each other without any words.

Andy El raised her eyebrow, as if asking a question, and then Raymond gave her a look filled with so much love, that it nearly broke what was left of my heart. He gave a tiny nod, and they smiled at each other, as though agreeing on something. Then Raymond drew himself up straight and tall and looked right at Mrs. Carlisle.

"I'm Truly's father," he announced calmly. "If you check the records, you'll find my name on Truly's birth certificate."

CHAPTER 31

I turned and ran.

Blindly, I tore down the hill past all of the trailers, through the Cut, and came out on the beach. My puppy ran joyously along beside me, yipping delightedly, ready to play.

No one was there. I threw myself down on a log, breathing heavily. I couldn't cry. I had no more tears. I just sat there shaking, my ears ringing, filled with rage. I felt even more betrayed than when Clarice had abandoned me.

All these years of wondering, and here Raymond was my mysterious father. He had never said anything to me. And he had abandoned me to live with Clarice, even though he knew what kind of a mother she had turned out to be. How could I have thought he was so nice?

I snuggled the puppy close and buried my face in his fur.

Raymond was my father. Not some mysterious stranger in Vancouver who loved Elvis. I just couldn't believe it. I sat there, absently petting the puppy, staring out at the ocean, watching the waves come crawling in and then sweep back out with a gentle swishing sound.

I don't know how long I sat there, but finally I got up, determined to find out just what was going on back at the trailer.

I stormed back up to the trailer in time to see the lady from Social Services drive off in her car. I stomped into the trailer. My puppy trailed in after me.

Raymond stood up from the couch as I came in.

I stormed over and stood in front of him, glaring, and said, "Is it true? You? You're my father?" and then I began punching him and yelling, over and over again. Raymond just stood there and let me hit him as I sobbed. I struck out about Clarice leaving me, taking my lemonade stand money, my whole sad, miserable life I had lived with Clarice for all these years. I kept hitting Raymond until I was spent and exhausted. I dropped to the floor and said dully, "So, now what happens? Is that lady going to take me away somewhere?"

Andy El helped me to my feet and sat me on the couch, holding me in her arms.

"You need to hear something. Something real important. You listen to Raymond, now. You hear every word he says, Truly," she said firmly to me.

I sat, glaring at him, and waited.

Raymond sighed and said, "I really wish I was your dad, Truly, but I'm not." Before I could speak, he held his hands up to stop me.

"I told that Social Services lady I was your dad so that you could stay here with Andy El, stay here with all of us. And after today, I will tell everyone that I really am your dad."

He stopped for a moment and then continued with a sad sigh.

"I knew your mom when she was in high school, Truly," he said. "She was a few years younger than me. She was real popular with a lot of boys, pretty wild, actually, but I never paid any attention to her, and I think that always bothered her. In fact, it drove her real crazy when a boy didn't pay attention to her. You see, that was all she had, being popular with boys." He stopped for a moment, and then continued.

"Mrs. Bateman, your grandmother, was always real hard on her. Clarice was always hounding me to take her out. And I just kept refusing. I just wasn't interested in Clarice. Her mom was real mean, and Clarice, well, Clarice was always getting into trouble. It was her way to rebel against her mother."

Raymond looked at me real gently. "I was never with your mom. When your mom got pregnant with you, I was away working, my first real job after high school. I was away working in a logging camp over on the mainland that year. And then in the fall, I went to college in Vancouver for a semester, till I got so homesick for the island that I came right back home. So there's no way that I really could be your dad."

"Then why —," I asked, but again Raymond held his hand up to shush me.

"When you were born, no one ever knew who your dad was. Oh, there were lots of guesses, but Clarice never would say who he was. And no one stepped forward to take responsibility for being your dad. I'm sorry, but that's the sad truth of it. But I do know that for some wild, crazy reason, when Clarice registered your birth, she put down my name — Raymond Joseph — on the birth certificate form as your father. She told Esther she did it, when you were a brand-new baby. And one night she got real drunk and told me the same thing. She laughed and said she did it out of spite. Because I was never interested in her."

He paused, and then said with a wry smile, "Well, there's lots of other Raymond Josephs around, you know. I know I got an uncle and a couple of cousins with the same name living up island. So, who knows, your father really could have been some other Raymond Joseph."

I didn't laugh. I didn't think it was funny.

Raymond continued. "The thing is, Truly, today I told

that lady that I really am your father, just like it says on your birth certificate. And today I even signed a bunch of government papers swearing that I am your dad. So that means that you can stay here with us. You can live here with Andy El at the trailer, and from now on, I'll help her raise you. I'll be your dad, and Andy El is now officially and legally your grandmother."

I stared at him. "You really did that for me?" I whispered.

Raymond grinned at me. "Well, the way I see it, the government says I'm an Indian because I got a card that says I am. In a way, it makes me an Indian on paper. I know lots of people who are Native, and for a bunch of different reasons, they don't get that paper. So, the government says they aren't really an Indian. Doesn't make a lot of sense, that some of us are Indians, and some of us aren't, just based on a government paper. So I figured, what the hell. If I can be a Government Paper Indian, I can be a Government Paper Dad, too."

"And I'm sorry, Truly. I guess I should have asked you if it was okay for me to tell that lady that I was your dad, but there honestly wasn't any time. That lady didn't give me any choice. She was gonna take you away from Andy El and all of us, maybe not today, but in a few days or weeks, and put you in a foster home. So I didn't have a lot of time to ask if it was okay with you. And it just seemed like the best thing to do.

"So," he paused, and said again, "I hope that's okay with you."

I just stared at him. Let it all sink in. Raymond had lied for me. Raymond had signed a form to say that he was my father, and that meant that Andy El was my real grandma. All of a sudden, finding my real dad didn't seem so important anymore.

"You really did that for me?" I said in wonder. "I can stay here now? For always? Mrs. Bateman can't have me sent away?"

Raymond grinned. "I did that for you, Truly, but I also did that for Andy El, and for all of us. If that Mrs. Carlisle had tried to take you away from here, I was getting real worried that Andy El was gonna punch that lady right in the nose! Then we'd have to bail her outta jail!"

CHAPTER 32

That night, I snuggled down in my bed with my puppy beside the bed in a cardboard box with an old towel folded in it. Andy El had tied an old sock into knots for a chew toy, to try to get him to stop chewing everything in sight.

"He'll learn, soon enough," said Andy El, patting his head.

Lately my life had been like riding on a roller coaster, but it seemed to be settling down into a routine.

Tomorrow, I decided, I was going to start the lemonade stand again. I was ready to face everyone, with all their questions. I would be proud to tell them that I was staying with Andy El and Raymond, for good. And I was going to need to earn money to look after my puppy.

So, early the next morning, I pulled out my stand and set it up, spreading out the tablecloth. I brought out the books and jars of jam, and then made up the first jug of lemonade, filling it with plenty of ice. I sat expectantly and waited for my first customer.

And that's when it happened. I should have known it was inevitable, really. Elvis left Eagle Shores.

I was sitting at my stand, reading my very last Miss Marple book, when he drove up in his gold Sun Bug. When he got out and came up to my stand, I could see that his car was filled with all his belongings. His guitar was carefully stowed on the back seat, and his suits hung in garment bags on the hooks behind the seats.

"You're leaving?" I asked. "For good?"

Elvis took off his aviator sunglasses and smiled down at me.

"Yeah, Truly, I am. But I figured that I better have one last glass of lemonade before I go," he said.

I poured the glass and handed it to him, my hand shaking. Not from nervousness this time. It was from sadness. Someone else was leaving me.

He took a sip and smiled. "Going to miss this, Truly. Nothin' finer than your lemonade." And he drained his glass.

"How come?" I asked. "How come you have to leave?"

He sighed and looked back at the line of trailers, and on past, down to the beach.

"Well, it's just time, I guess. You see, I got a real good opportunity to do some touring across Canada, and even down into the United States. So, for the next year or so, I'll be on the road so much that I won't be getting back to

Vancouver Island for a long while." He grinned at me and winked. "I'm gonna be the very best Elvis Presley tribute artist out there."

When he saw the stricken look on my face, he said, "But I'll be back, one day. I promise, Truly."

I couldn't help it. My lip trembled, and a tear slipped down my cheek.

Elvis smiled gently down at me. "You know, Truly, I want to tell you a secret." He looked around, to make sure that we were really alone. Mrs. Williams was clipping her roses, but she was well out of earshot. No one else was about.

I stared at him. This was it. He was going to tell me the truth, that he was the real Elvis Presley. And why he had come to Eagle Shores Trailer Park.

"Did you ever notice that when I wear my big flashy belts on stage, they all have 'TCB' on the buckles? Up till now, that's always stood for 'Taking Care of Business.' But from now on, just between you and me, whenever I put on one of my belts, it's gonna stand for 'Truly Clarice Bateman.' That's for someone special, someone that I consider a real special friend."

I just stared at him like an idiot.

"For a real good friend, one who can keep a secret and be loyal to the end," he added.

And then he said in a real serious voice, "You know, Truly,

I have lived a real blessed life. I've had some real good luck in my life, and I've suffered through some real hard times, too." He paused, and then continued. "For a while there, when things was goin' real good for me, I ended up surrounded by people who thought they knew what was best for me, and I let them all start tellin' me what to do. They made it all so easy. After a while, I realized that I had just … kind of lost control of who I really was inside. And I discovered that I wasn't happy with who I had become. So one day, I just packed my bags and walked away from that life. And I set out to find just who I really am. And I found it, right here at Eagle Shores." He grinned at me.

"And one thing I learned from all of that is this: you gotta just set one foot in front of the other, keep goin', and look for the good in life. Don't let people tell you how to live or control how you feel. No matter where you come from, it doesn't matter, because you can always choose where you're goin'. And nobody can take that away from you. You hang on to that. And I figure that right here, right now, you got the very best there is with Andy El, and Raymond, and Esther and her family. I know that your mama ran out on you, but you got a whole family right here. A family that loves you and will keep you safe."

I realized that he was right. All along, I had had a family right here, looking after me and caring for me. And now, it was official. I had a real dad, and a grandma too in Andy El, who had always loved me like her own granddaughter.

He held out his hand and shook mine.

“I promise, I’ll try to come back one day to see you again, Truly Clarice Bateman.” With that, he got into his Bug and drove away with a wave of his hand.

Elvis had left the Trailer Park.

CHAPTER 33

And so, we settled into a routine at the trailer, Andy El and me. Raymond — my new dad — comes over nearly every day to see how we're doing, and has supper with us. He's starting to teach me things, like how to clean fish and set them up to smoke them, and he's going to take me out fishing in the bay real soon.

I started calling Esther "Auntie Esther." I think she likes that. I know I do. She teased me the first time I did it and said, "As long as you don't call me 'Andy Es' — you'll make me sound like a snake!"

Agnes and Linda are now my cousins. It feels a bit strange. It feels good. We'll be going to school together next year, at the junior high school in town, so I will have two friends right there with me. They'll ride the bus from Eagle Shores with me, too.

And you know what? I spent my whole summer desperate to save my lemonade stand money to go find my real dad, knowing that he was somewhere in Vancouver and I could just get on a ferry and go find him. Desperate to chase some dream. And now it doesn't seem to matter anymore. I don't need to know who my mysterious dad is. Because now Raymond is my forever dad. And Andy El is my grandmother. And I realized that this whole time I have had a whole built-in family, right here at Eagle Shores. A family who loves me, and who makes sure that I am included. And who knows if my real dad would even want to meet me?

I still set up the lemonade stand every day, and I even added some jars of blackberry jam for sale, and Mrs. Marshall's muffins that she still likes to give me to sell.

Even though I didn't need to pay for my puppy, and I'm not going to Vancouver now, I still wanted to help out Andy El with buying dog food, and stuff for me.

Andy El and Raymond got together with Esther one evening, and they planned a whole day's outing for us to get some supplies and new clothes for school.

So on a Saturday a week before school was to start, we all went together into Victoria to shop at the Woolco store, and Andy El and Raymond bought me a pair of new shoes, two pairs of jeans, and some new tops, and even a new winter coat. Esther had the list of school supplies we needed, and she and Andy El filled a shopping cart with all of the notebooks, binders, pencils, and other things that we would all need for the school year.

And then Raymond treated us all to lunch at the lunch counter in Woolco. Agnes and Linda and I sat on the red counter stools, spinning back and forth until we were dizzy, until our plates of fish and chips and mugs of root beer arrived. Andy El sat with Raymond and Esther at a booth, and they ate their lunch, keeping a watchful eye on us girls.

That was something new for me, something that'll take some time for me to get used to. I am not at all used to planning ahead more than one day at a time, or getting new clothes and stuff when I need them. It was the best day ever.

I got into a routine of getting up early every morning and taking my puppy out for a little walk, and then feeding him in his special bowl. He'd already learned to sit and stay, and he was working on walking on the leash instead of grabbing it and wrestling for it.

The night before school started, Andy El and I hosted one last hot dog roast to celebrate the end of summer. Raymond came over, as well as Auntie Esther and the twins. As we sat by the fire, I showed off my puppy's tricks for them all.

"Whatever are you going to name that puppy?" asked Andy El. "He needs a good name."

Raymond nodded, grinning at me, "Yeah, Truly — having the right name is real important, I've always found." That made us all laugh, real hard.

Up until now I hadn't settled on a name for my puppy. I hadn't been able to name him. And at that moment I realized why. Somehow, I had still been convinced that my puppy would be taken away from me and that I wouldn't be able to keep him after all. Deep down I felt that it would be easier for me if I hadn't given him a name. It would mean that I wasn't really close to him, and it would be easier to let him go.

But he really was mine. I would never have to give him up. Just like Andy El and Raymond, and my whole family. And that's when it came to me, the perfect name for the puppy.

I looked up at everyone and said, "I've got it! His name is Elvis!" When he heard it, my puppy came trotting over and licked my hand enthusiastically.

"Elvis, sit!" I said. He did, promptly.

Everyone laughed. "Looks like he knows it already," said Raymond.

Andy El looked at me with such love and pride that I wanted to burst.

"It's a perfect name," she said. "Now, Elvis will always be with us right here at Eagle Shores!"

ACKNOWLEDGEMENTS

I am indebted to Barry Jowett of Cormorant/DCB for believing in this book, and for guiding me through the editing process, along with Sarah Jensen and Andrea Waters. You made me mine deep and make this a far better story than it would have been without your skill and vision. My gratitude to Sarah Cooper for helping me navigate the dotting of T's and crossing of I's to make the legal stuff happen, all with such grace and humour.

I have been honoured and blessed to have been mentored by some great authors along the way. I count you among my dearest friends and teachers. Linda Rogers, who gave so freely of her time and wisdom, many, many thanks to you. Sylvia Olsen, so much laughter and sage advice through the years, I thank you. Karen Lee White, author and big sister who nagged incessantly to keep me writing everyday. I am loathe to admit it, but you were right. And now it's here in print.

This book would not have been written without the generous love and support of my husband, Dan Gentile, who gave me all of the time and space I needed to create Truly and tell her story. My children Aimes Gentile & Alwyn Crocker, Lyse Gentile & Tanner Exelby, Tristan & Lisa Gentile, who have always believed that this would happen one day, and kept me working and dreaming.

My friend Glenda Kohse, who read the first drafts and gave me so much support and encouragement. My longtime friend Carla Wilson, who always believed I had it in me. My big brother and my hero Douglas White, who showed my how to fly with the eagles.

My nieces and nephews, who always loved my stories. I cherish that gift of a day years ago when we sat in Portage Park and you asked me to tell more and still more of my stories. You even tried to tell me the wrong time, to keep me there telling more tales. It was magic, and you inspired me to keep writing.

To my other siblings and my greater community of family and friends, I am blessed to have you all in my life, and I raise my hands to you. Thank you.

Leslie Gentile is a singer/songwriter of Indigenous and settler heritage. She performs with her children in The Leslie Gentile Band, and with one of her sisters in The Half White Band. Gentile currently lives on Vancouver island with her husband. *Elvis, Me, and the Lemonade Stand Summer* is her first novel.

We acknowledge the sacred land on which Cormorant Books operates. It has been a site of human activity for 15,000 years. This land is the territory of the Huron-Wendat and Petun First Nations, the Seneca, and most recently, the Mississaugas of the Credit River. The territory was the subject of the Dish With One Spoon Wampum Belt Covenant, an agreement between the Iroquois Confederacy and Confederacy of the Ojibway and allied nations to peaceably share and steward the resources around the Great Lakes. Today, the meeting place of Toronto is still home to many Indigenous people from across Turtle Island. We are grateful to have the opportunity to work in the community, on this territory.

We are also mindful of broken covenants and the need to strive to make right with all our relations.